WHILE SHE SLEPT

A PSYCHOLOGICAL SUSPENSE THRILLER

N. L. HINKENS

Text copyright @ 2023 Norma Hinkens

Published by Dunecadia Publishing, California

ISBN: 978-1-947890-41-1

Cover by: https://www.derangeddoctordesign.com/

Editing by: https://www.jeanette-morris.com/first-impressions-writing/

1

When I wake up on the first day of our honeymoon, I expect Declan to be lying here next to me whispering "Good morning, Mrs. Cafferty," in my ear, his easy grin spreading across his face as he rubs his goatee against my cheek before smothering me with kisses. But when I stretch out my hand to find him, his side of the bed is cool to the touch.

A flicker of disappointment stirs inside me, but I'm determined not to begin the day irritated that he's gone out for an early morning run and left me to sleep in. It's not as if we're co-dependent teenagers, and this isn't a first marriage for either of us. Declan made it clear from the outset how important his training schedule is to him. He's been looking forward to pounding the leafy, country roads around the idyllic Airbnb cottage we rented in County Clare on the west coast of Ireland.

I yawn and stretch my arms lazily over my head, admiring my new wedding band as I try to decide if I'm ready to roll out of bed and make myself a large mug of coffee. My thoughts turn to work, as they usually do first thing in the morning, but it's too early to check in with my assistant, Maddie. It's only 1:00 a.m. in Los Angeles where I work as a controller for a technology company.

I'm one of those fortunate people who love their job. It kept me sane when I lost my first husband, Eric, to an aggressive colon cancer four years ago—a dark, surreal time when all my dreams were abruptly put through a shredder. I never imagined when I was walking down the aisle that the expiration date would come so soon. Eric and I were soulmates. It's not the kind of relationship you can easily go out and replace—more like the kind people die of a broken heart from—which made it all the more remarkable when Declan came into my life.

Stop it, Abby! I rub my face vigorously to rid myself of any lingering thoughts of loss. Those memories have no claim on me today. I'm spending my honeymoon in the beautiful Emerald Isle—no longer a widow, but a bride, once again. I'm ready to embrace my new reality and let go of the pain I've clung to during too many long, lonely nights, as silence echoed off the walls of my house.

Today, I have new memories to make. I smile to myself as I plump up my pillow, recalling the intimate wedding ceremony Declan and I planned down to the last detail, attended only by family and a few close friends. It was everything I hoped it would be. Well, almost everything. Declan's sixteen-year-old adopted daughter, Brynn, was a somewhat reluctant maid of honor, if I'm being honest.

We did everything we could to make her feel as much a part of our new family as possible—including a commitment to love her in our marriage vows. Brynn is the only child I will ever have, and I intend to honor my promise to her. I even landed on the idea of sharing the phoenix, a mythological bird endowed with longevity and characterized by its power to be reborn from its ashes, as our family symbol of hope and new beginnings. We gifted Brynn a fourteen-karat gold ring with the bird embossed into it, I chose a necklace, and Declan got a phoenix tattoo on his leg. Brynn seemed to buy into the idea at the time, but I noticed she wasn't wearing her ring at the ceremony. It could have been a gesture of defiance, but it wasn't worth bringing up and risking an argument over. Maybe she felt it was disloyal to her deceased mother.

With a final contented stretch, I whisk back the duvet and swing my legs over the edge of the bed to peer through the crack in the curtains at the vibrant rolling countryside. I get to my feet and plod across the wooden floorboards to take in the view. The undulating fields are blanketed in a plush green, the kind of saturation you only ever see in a land kissed by rain on a near daily basis. The morning sun eases its way through scattered clouds, its rays electrifying the lush mantle of grass below. In the distance, I can make out the faint outline of a rainbow, and my grin widens. It's a good sign on the first day of our ten-day honeymoon—not that I have any need of the fabled pot of gold at the end of a rainbow. I have Declan.

At the creak of the front door opening, my mood instantly elevates at the thought of my new husband's return and a day spent exploring the soaring cliffs and sandy beaches. Kneeling by my suitcase, I rummage around for a sweater to throw over my shoulders. Despite the promise of blue skies, April in Ireland is not particularly warm. Maybe we'll find a pub with a roaring fire and some traditional Irish music to while away a few hours in this evening.

"Hello? Anyone home?" a female voice sings out.

I get to my feet, my mood deflating a fraction.

"Be right there!" I call back, as I wrestle my arms into my sweater and pull it over my head.

Moira Murphy, the woman who owns the Airbnb, is standing in the front doorway holding aloft a plate of freshly baked goodies. My stomach rumbles as a delicate blend of flaky scones and rich butter wafts my way.

"Morning Abby. I thought you lovebirds might enjoy a wee scone for breakfast. The door was ajar, or I would have left them on the bench outside. I brought you some soda bread too." She wipes a hand on her apron self-consciously as her eyes travel over my pajama bottoms. "I hope I didn't wake you."

I swat a hand through the air, making a mental note to remind Declan to lock the door behind him when he leaves. "Not at all. I was having a lazy morning. My husband must have left the door unlatched. He took off for an early run."

Moira raises her brows, as if she's not sure what to make of that. I hope she doesn't think he stormed out after an argument and I'm making up an excuse to cover for his absence.

"He's training for a marathon in San Jose this fall," I explain, pasting on a bright smile. "He has to run a set amount of miles every day."

"Oh aye." Moira gives a knowing nod. "My cousin's daughter ran in the London marathon last year. She trains on the beach all the time, rain or shine. Is that where your Declan went?"

I give a nonchalant shrug. "I'm not sure. He might be running on the road."

Moira sets the plate of scones and soda bread on a small table just inside the door and gives me a circumspect look. "I wouldn't advise it. The young folks drive way too fast in these parts." She purses her lips and gives a disapproving shake of her head. "There was a fellah last year knocked down a young mother pushing her baby in a pram. Killed the wee one and left the mother in a wheelchair. Drivers don't take a blind bit of notice."

I tug at my sweater sleeve, digesting the information. I'm not overly concerned. Declan knows what he's doing—he lived in Ireland until his parents divorced when he was twelve. Still, no sense in upsetting Moira by being cavalier about it. She seems the type to fluster easily, despite her jovial manner. "He probably went to the beach," I reassure her. "I'm sure he'll be back any minute."

Moira gives a mollified nod. "If you need anything at all, come on up to the house and knock on the back door. The pub lunches are very good around here, but I'd avoid O'Connell's if I were you. The waitress there is a right rude cow."

I suppress a smile and thank Moira for the baked goods. She takes her leave and makes her way back up the lane to the old farmhouse where she lives with her husband, Cormac, and their twenty-something-year-old son, Shane.

Apparently, Shane has no interest in moving out, getting married, or giving them grandchildren—any of which Moira would be grateful for, but deems unlikely due to him being a bit soft in the head—whatever that means. Declan and I learned all this yesterday when we stopped by to pick up the key to the cottage. Reading between the lines, I get the impression that Shane has never had a real job. Even though I don't know these people, it bothers me that he's a grown man sponging off his parents. It's not as if they're rolling in money. The stone cottage we're staying in was originally built as a shed to store farm implements, and Moira and Cormac told us they renovated it and rent it out to supplement their income.

I take my time unpacking and enjoy a leisurely shower before brewing a pot of coffee and sitting down at the kitchen table. My entire body melts with pleasure when I take a bite of one of Moira's scones slathered in Kerrygold butter. Declan is missing out. The best time to eat these is when they're fresh. I glance at the time on my phone, shocked to see that it's almost 11:30 a.m. Despite my best intentions, I'm starting to get ticked off. I know we agreed he would keep up his rigorous training schedule, but I thought that meant he would go running early in the mornings and we would spend the days together. It's almost lunchtime—he could have run a marathon by now.

My thoughts drift back to what Moira said about the roads around here. A niggling feeling of disquiet stirs in my belly. I hope nothing's happened to him. From now on, I'm going to insist he take his phone with him. I don't care if I have to strap it to his forehead. I need to know where he is. I'm his wife, and we're alone in a foreign country, after all.

I munch my way through two scones and consume a second cup of coffee, alternating between fuming at Declan and worrying about him. I take my time washing my mug and plate, before making the decision to take our rental car and go out and look for him. I scribble a quick note and leave it on the kitchen table in case he comes back in the meantime.

With an air of apprehension, I slide in behind the wheel of the VW Golf we rented. Moira's horror story about the young mother pushing her baby in a pram plays on a loop in my head. What if I end up mowing Declan down on a blind corner? I've never driven on the other side of the road before, and I've only used a stick shift once when I was dating a guy in college who had a souped-up Mustang with a manual transmission.

Just when I've psyched myself up enough to start the car, I spot Cormac striding down the lane with a walking stick and two collie dogs bounding along at his heels. I give him a quick wave to get his attention before climbing out.

"Morning!" I call to him, hoping my voice doesn't sound too strained. "I don't suppose you've seen Declan, by chance?"

Cormac walks over to me, rubbing his chin thoughtfully. "No, can't say I have."

"He went out running but he hasn't come back, yet. I was just about to go looking for him."

Cormac grunts. "Running, eh? Wouldn't be one bit wise on these roads. Did you try the pub? First place my wife would look." He lets out a hearty chuckle and the dogs start barking in response.

I smile politely. *The pub, seriously? It's not even noon.* "He might have gone to the beach. Can you give me some directions?"

"You'll want to take a left when you get out to the main road and then a right at the junction. You'll see the sign for White Strand. It's only two kilometers from there."

"Great, thank you."

Cormac twists his walking stick in his hand, a deep trough forming on his brow. "He wouldn't want to be running on the cliff top trail. Folks love the view from up there, but that wind has a mind of its own—take the feet right out from under you, it will. Couple of years back it blew a caravan into the sea. Two wee kids died."

My hand flutters to my chest as I take in Cormac's sober expression. He isn't chuckling anymore. Anxiety is mounting inside me. I can't pretend there isn't at least a possibility that something has happened to Declan. "I

7

should get going," I mumble, reaching for the car door handle.

"Would you be needing some help?" Cormac gestures over his shoulder. "Shane there could drive you. He knows these roads like the back of his hand."

I glance up and meet the hollowed-out stare of a greasy-haired man leaning back against a cattle gate.

2
_____

A tingling sensation creeps over my shoulders as the man continues to gape unabashedly at me. So this is the infamous Shane. I'd built up a picture of him in my mind as a socially awkward, grown man who'd never cut the apron strings. But the vibe I'm getting from him is altogether different. His intrusive stare sends a shiver through me.

I turn my attention back to Cormac. "Thank you," I manage to squeak out. "That won't be necessary. I'll take a quick drive around myself. I'm sure Declan will show up before long. He might have got lost on these winding roads."

Without waiting for Cormac's response, I climb back inside the rental car and start the engine. Thankfully, I make it out of the driveway without stalling, but changing gears proves trickier and the car jerks forward in response to my muddled efforts. I do my best to avoid looking in Shane's direction. I have a sneaking suspicion I'll be met with a smirk as I crawl slowly down the lane toward the main road. My pulse races as I anticipate navigating the unfamiliar, narrow roads and oncoming traffic, all the while juggling the mechanics of a stick shift and my conflicting emotions.

I make it halfway to the junction Cormac talked about before seeing another vehicle. It's a huge Massey Ferguson tractor trundling along at a snail's pace in front of me, kicking up clods of dirt in its wake. My heartbeat ratchets up a notch when the friendly farmer inside sticks out a burly arm and waves me by. There's no oncoming traffic in sight, but the next blind corner looks too close for comfort to an inexperienced stick shifter like me. A quick glance in my rearview mirror reveals a delivery truck on my bumper, and another car closing in behind. I can't sit here like a dork any longer holding everyone up. I turn on the blinker and accelerate, too busy clenching the steering wheel and the gear shift to wave my thanks to the farmer. A relieved breath slips through my lips when I make it safely past the monstrous tractor.

Minutes later, I pull into a parking spot at the beach. I waste no time clambering out, inhaling the salty tang of the ocean as I jog down to the sand. A cursory scan of the beach shows no sign of Declan, but the strand stretches as far as the eye can see in both directions. It's dotted with dog walkers, clusters of people paddling in the water, and kids playing in the sand. Pulling out my phone, I scroll through to a recent picture of Declan, before approaching a couple walking back to their car. "Excuse me," I say, interrupting their blissful oblivion to the outside world. They blink, heads turning in tandem in my direction.

"I'm looking for my husband," I say, holding my phone out in front of them. They peer curiously at Declan's picture. "We just arrived here yesterday and we're staying at an Airbnb nearby. My husband went out for a run this morning and I think he might have gotten lost." I give a sheepish chuckle. "We're still a bit jet lagged."

The woman glances at her partner and then shrugs apologetically before shaking her head. "Sorry, we haven't seen him. Do you want us to call you if we bump into him?"

"Sure, that would be great," I reply, touched by her offer, although I doubt it will come to anything. I rattle off my name and number and the woman types it into her phone.

The pair wander off, gazing at each other, arms entwined. I don't hold out much hope of them noticing Declan even if he were to run right past them naked.

My thoughts go back to the first time I set eyes on him. He was running, of course, at the park. I was walking my dog, Aspen, when she took off after a squirrel, leash trailing, tripping him up in the process. He agreed to accept my profuse apologies if I met him for lunch the following day. We ended up spending the whole afternoon together, drinking a boatload of coffee, and walking around town until my feet ached. That's when he told me about the tragic death of his wife.

"Our marriage wasn't in a good place at the time," he'd admitted, toying with his coffee cup. "We had a huge argument that day and she stormed out of the house—didn't say where she was going. It was the last time I saw her. She took our boat out on the lake and a fisherman found it capsized the following day." He grimaced, pain etched across his face. "They never found her body, just one of her shoes that washed up on shore."

"Declan, I'm so sorry," I'd said, awkwardly clutching his hand.

"To make matters worse, the police suspected I might have had something to do with it," he went on. "We'd been fighting. I'd accused Lynelle of having an affair. She denied it, but she was hiding something from me. She was with-drawn—seemed depressed. To be honest, I've always wondered if she committed suicide." He tugged a hand through his hair and sighed. "I guess I'll never know."

"How on earth did you get through it all?"

"Brynn, our daughter," he'd said, his face brightening as he pulled up a picture of her on his phone. "We adopted her when she was six weeks old. If it hadn't been for her, I don't think I could have kept going."

It had taken Brynn some time to get used to the idea that her father was going to remarry. Her attitude softened some-what after I asked her to be my maid of honor, but she still resents me to some degree. I'm under no illusions about the fact that it will take some adjustment starting a new life together as a family once the honeymoon is over. It can't be easy for Brynn. She was only thirteen years old when she lost her mother. I know I can never replace her but maybe, in time, I can help fill the void.

By the time I've walked all the way across the beach to the rock pools on the west side, I'm dehydrated and deflated. I've talked to everyone I crossed paths with, but no one has seen Declan.

"If you like, I could call the gardaí for you?" a concerned woman offers, one eye on the toddler at her feet who's busy slapping at the sand with a plastic shovel.

I stare blankly at her.

"The *police*," she says with emphasis, interpreting my silence as confusion.

"Oh, yes," I say, scratching my forehead as I consider her offer. "I ... I don't know if that's necessary, yet." I can't help picturing the look of embarrassment on Declan's face if the police should happen upon him sharing a pint at a pub with an old childhood friend, or something equally benign. "I'll hold off a little longer," I tell her. "It's possible my husband bumped into someone he knew and got waylaid. He lived around here as a child."

"Ah sure, he's probably getting his ear talked off, in that case! He'll turn up before long," the woman replies, turning her attention back to her whimpering child who has rubbed sand in his eyes.

Back in the rental car, I lay my head on the steering wheel and try to collect my thoughts. I'm suddenly feeling emotionally drained and lonely. It feels like I'm losing Eric all over again. With a drawn-out groan, I straighten up and start the engine. I can't let myself go back to that dark place. No sense in jumping the gun and torturing myself with what-ifs that might never transpire. It's not even that late, yet—it's only lunchtime. There's likely a perfectly simple explanation for Declan's absence. He might have sprained his ankle and be waiting on a Good Samaritan to find him. As I put the car in gear, I decide to drive up top and check out the cliff trail Cormac mentioned. If Declan is injured, it could be a while before someone discovers him up there.

Moments later, I pull into the small cliff top parking area that services the hiking trail. The view out over the ocean is breathtaking, but the second I open the car door, the wind blows it wide open, almost wrenching it off its hinges. The brochures I picked up at the airport are sucked out and take flight before I can grab hold of them. I watch them flapping their way toward the edge of the cliffs. I'm not stupid enough to try and retrieve them. One gust could pick me up and send me hurtling down to the ocean in half a heartbeat. My shoulders shake as the bracing wind cuts through me. I could really use the down jacket I left behind at the cottage.

With some difficulty, I manage to slam the car door shut and make my way on foot to the trailhead. Thankfully, there's a good twenty feet between the trail and the edge of the cliffs, as well as a small two-foot metal barrier and a warning sign advising visitors of the high winds and the risks of standing too close to the edge. As I walk along the path, I keep my muscles clenched, ready to take my stand against any moves to take me down by the biting cold wind. Unsurprisingly, I don't see anyone else on the trail, but there were a couple of vehicles in the parking lot. If I keep walking, maybe I'll bump into someone who might have seen Declan. It's too windy to run along this trail but he might have come up to check out the view. My stomach knots as I picture the worst-case scenario: his broken body lying on the rocks below. If Cormac is to be believed, it wouldn't be the first time a tourist plummeted to their death courtesy of the gnarly Atlantic winds.

I glance up at the hum of voices. Rounding a corner I spot a small group of Japanese tourists clustered around a scenic viewpoint. They're dressed appropriately for the weather in matching navy Snow Peak windbreakers, accessorized with a plethora of camera equipment and iPads.

"Excuse-me!" I call to them, my voice scarcely audible in the wind even to my own ears. I jog over to the group and give them my best attempt at a disarming smile as they turn their befuddled attention to me. If their startled expressions are anything to go by, they think they're about to be robbed.

"I'm looking for my husband," I blurt out, holding out my phone and stabbing a finger at the picture of Declan. "Have you seen him?"

I shift impatiently from one foot to the other as they pass the phone around, exchanging snippets of conversation. Finally, one of the group replies in halting English. "No, sorry. No see him."

My gaze travels over the rest of the group. One-by-one, they shake their heads, their expressions blank.

"Thanks," I say, pocketing my phone. "I'll keep looking."

Disheartened, I turn back. I'll drive around the roads for a bit and see if I can spot him. It's possible he took a wrong turn and ended up running for miles in the opposite direction. That would explain why it's taking him so long to get back to the cottage.

I stuff my hands into the pockets of my jeans for warmth as I duck into the wind and head back toward the parking lot. I'm still holding out hope that there's a simple explanation for Declan's disappearance. There has to be. The alternative doesn't bear thinking about. My heart shudders in my chest.

What am I going to tell Brynn if I'm wrong?

3

---

t the junction where I had turned to go to White Strand Beach, I pull over and retrieve a map of the area from the glove box. It's one of those colorful brochures detailing all the local tourist attractions, but most of the roads aren't labeled and it's not to scale, which makes it next to useless. I suppose I could use the GPS on my phone, but I have no idea where I want to go. I might as well just keep driving in the opposite direction and see where the road takes me. The compass in the rental car tells me I'm heading due east. As long as I can find my way back to this junction, I'll be fine.

As I drive, I can't help but be awed by the jaw-dropping scenery. The country roads are winding tunnels of green with arched hedges practically meeting in the middle. It's Lord-of-the-Rings ethereal, but it makes for hazardous driving. There are more cars on the road now, and my eyes are beginning to feel like they're in a pinball machine— dashing between blind corners and hedgerows to the unfamiliar controls in the rental car. Surely Declan wouldn't have gone running on these roads? It's far too dangerous.

My nerves are fraying like string when it suddenly occurs to me that he doesn't have any ID on him. If he's been knocked unconscious, and taken to hospital, they won't even know who to call.

A tour bus looms large on the upcoming bend, so I tuck the car as far into the hedge as I can possibly go without sinking the wheels in the soggy ditch. My breathing stills as the bus closes the gap between us. Miraculously, it glides by within a hairsbreadth of the rental car. The driver gives a casual wave, acknowledging my efforts to give him space. My pulse is still thundering in my ears as I pull back out onto the road and continue driving, all the while keeping an eye out for Declan. The reality is, he'll be hard to spot if he's lying in a ditch somewhere—everything is so overgrown. To make matters worse, the clouds have coagulated into a gray mass, and it's beginning to spit rain.

Fumbling to find the windshield wipers, I flinch at the sound of a horn blaring behind me. I glance in my rearview mirror and spot a truck hugging my bumper. I edge to the left, hoping I don't scrape the door panel on the crumbling stone wall flanking the road. The truck flashes its lights in thanks and whips around the bend in front of me. I continue driving for another few miles before rounding a corner and almost careening into a cow that's wandered into the middle of the road. Slamming on the brakes, I skid to a halt in the ditch, vibrating with shock. I watch in astonishment as a ruddy-faced farmer pedals into view. He yells something unintelligible at the cow and shoos it until it plods obediently through an open cattle gate into an adjacent field. I turn off the engine, trembling all over. I have no idea if the car's still drivable, but my brain's too filled with static to operate a vehicle anyway.

A sharp knock on the window startles me. Uncertain of

my reception, I roll down the window an inch or two. I'm not sure how sacred cows are in Ireland, or who has the right of way, but at least I didn't hit the animal. The most the pedaling farmer can chew me out for is traumatizing Bessie.

"All right, are ye?" he asks, peering out from under a tweed flat cap.

"I ... yes, I'm fine, thanks. Just a little shook up."

"You're American," he remarks, rubbing his chin.

It's not exactly a question so I nod and give a pinched smile. "My husband and I are renting an Airbnb nearby. I'm Abby Cafferty."

"Thomas Doyle." He glances at the map lying open on the passenger seat. "Are ye lost?"

I try to chuckle politely, but it sounds more like I'm choking back a sob. "*I'm* not, but I think my husband might be."

Thomas scratches the back of his neck as I proceed to explain the situation as briefly as possible. "I don't know what to do. He didn't take his phone with him. We're staying at the Murphys' Airbnb a few miles down the road."

Thomas nods. "I know Cormac and Moira well. I'll ring them up and ask them to give ye a lift back. You're in no state to drive." He frowns up at the sky. "It'll be bucketing down here in a minute."

"What about my car?" I ask.

"I'll have my Jimmy bring the tractor over the field and get you out." He bends down and inspects the front bumper. "No harm done. Only a bit of mud that'll need hosing off."

He pulls out a phone and, a moment later, I hear him conversing rapidly with someone in a thick brogue that sounds nothing like the conversation I had with him. When he's finished making calls, he bends down and peers through the window again. "All taken care of. Jimmy's firing up the tractor and Cormac will be on his way as soon as he finishes moving the sheep."

"I can't tell you how much I appreciate your help," I say.

"Ah, you're grand," he says, "Sure it's my fault you're in the ditch to begin with."

I look up at the sound of a tractor motoring across the field to my rescue. Within minutes of his arrival on the scene, the intrepid Jimmy manages to nudge all four wheels of my car back onto the road. He has just taken off again when a beat-up blue Toyota Corolla cruises into view and slows to a stop by the cattle gate.

My relief is short-lived when I see who's sitting in the passenger seat next to Cormac.

4

_____

"I'm sorry to drag you away from your work," I say, when Cormac steps out of the car.

"No bother at all," he replies. "Thomas said you were awful shook up." He gestures with his chin to Shane who's stubbing out a cigarette in the dirt with his boot. "Shane's offered to drive your rental back for you."

I fight to keep my expression neutral. "That's ... very kind of him. Should I ride with you in that case?"

Cormac gives an amused snort. "Not unless you want to reek of manure. My car's a right mess. Best get a lift with Shane."

I glance in Shane's direction, but he's peering off into the distance, acting as if he hasn't heard a word we've said, even though I know he's been listening intently—just like his eyes were drilling into me earlier. He makes my skin crawl, but it appears my only choice is to ride back to the cottage with him, or drive myself, which I don't feel up to, especially not in this downpour. I don't know why I'm baulking at the prospect. It's not as if Shane's likely to attack me in the short drive back to the cottage. Still, I don't relish the thought of spending even a few minutes alone with him. Something about him disturbs me, and I've never been one to ignore a gut feeling.

I climb into the passenger seat of the VW Golf and plug in my seatbelt, grateful to be out of the rain. Shane starts the car and expertly executes a three-point turn. I grip the sides of the seat as he shoots off down the road at a speed that is nothing short of reckless. Knowing the roads like the back of his hand is one thing, anticipating what's around the next corner is a roll of the dice.

"S-s-some honeymoon, eh?" Shane remarks, breaking the jagged silence between us.

I glance across at him, searching for any hint of amusement in his eyes, but his face is contorted in an expression of pain. Does he actually feel sorry for me? I can't help but feel touched at the thought. Have I misjudged him? Maybe he's not a shirker, and his stutter has prevented him from getting a job.

"It's been a bit of a rough start," I concede, turning to look out the window. "Things can only get better. Thankfully, the car seems to be none the worse for wear, and I'm sure Declan will show up soon. He probably got lost and hitched a ride with someone now that it's raining. These roads all look the same and there's not much signage once you get off the main drag."

Shane throws me a puzzled look but says nothing. Easy for him—he grew up here, and I dare say he hasn't ventured far since.

My stomach rumbles, reminding me I've had nothing to eat since Moira's scones this morning. I glance at the time and suck in a sharp breath. How can it be 3:30 p.m. already?

Declan could have completed *two* marathons by now. My thoughts gravitate once more to Brynn. The idea of having to break the news to her that her father is missing sends daggers through me. It's worse than telling her he's at the hospital with a broken leg or something. At least then we'd know what we were dealing with. The not knowing is unbearable.

"Sh-sh-she h-handled well," Shane mumbles, as we pull into the cottage driveway and park.

"Thank you so much for driving me back," I reply, hurriedly making my exit.

Shane jumps out of the car and fixes a piercing stare on me as I walk up to the front door. "Wh-what'll you do n-n-now?" he calls after me, stuffing his hands into his pockets.

"I'm going to call the hospital, and then contact the gardaí."

Shane shuffles awkwardly from one foot to the other. "N-n-no need."

I grip the handle of my purse tightly. "Obviously, something's happened to my husband. I'm sure the gardaí will take the fact that we're not locals into consideration and help me search for him."

I glance up at the rumble of the Toyota Corolla coming back down the lane. Cormac pulls in next to my rental and turns off the ignition.

An apron-clad Moira spills out, clutching a bulging grocery bag. "Oh, Abby, I'm so sorry!" she sputters, throwing a doughy arm around me and squeezing me before ushering me inside. "I'm sending Cormac and Shane to ask around if any of the neighbors have seen Declan. What can I do to help you in the meantime?"

"Well, I was just about to call the hospitals," I say.

"Have you had a bite to eat at all?" Moira asks, abruptly turning the conversation to food as she sets about unpacking the groceries on the counter.

"I had two of your delicious scones this morning."

She tuts her disapproval. "That'll hardly tide you over. I'll put the kettle on and make you a wee sandwich."

"Thank you," I say sinking down on a kitchen chair. I pull out my phone and start Googling local hospitals. "I suppose I should begin with the closest ones," I say, looking to Moira for her input.

"You might try Ennis and Limerick too," she suggests. "They'll have taken him there if he has any serious injuries."

In between phone calls, I manage to swallow a few bites of a chicken sandwich made with Moira's mouthwatering soda bread. But, with each dead end I run into, my appetite wanes until I finally push the plate to one side. "Your bread's amazing, Moira, but I can't eat another bite. My stomach's churning with anxiety."

"You poor dear," she exclaims. "I suppose it's good news that none of the hospitals have admitted him."

"Maybe, maybe not," I say dubiously. "I think it's time I called the gardaí."

FORTY-FIVE MINUTES LATER, I'm seated in the cottage's tiny open plan kitchen and family room across from Garda Walsh, a balding man in his fifties with a fleshy nose and ruddy complexion, and Garda Doyle, a thin-lipped younger man with gelled back ginger hair. I waste no time bringing them up to speed on everything that's transpired and what I've done so far in an attempt to locate Declan. "I'd still be out there looking for him if I hadn't driven into the ditch," I say. "Shane was kind enough to drive the car back to the cottage for me."

Walsh raises his brows at that but makes no comment. "Can I see a picture of your husband?" he asks.

I pull out my phone and scroll through to the same photo I've been using all day. It's a favorite of mine—Declan relaxing in a deck chair, his genial smile aimed at the camera, his salt-and-pepper hair combed away from his face and flopping slightly to one side, his neatly-trimmed graying goatee chic on his rugged jaw.

"Airdrop that to me, would you?" Walsh says.

"You mentioned that your husband grew up here," Doyle pipes up. "Does he have any family in the area?"

I shake my head. "His parents are dead and his sister lives in Los Angeles. He hasn't lived here since he was twelve. He had a couple of cousins who lived in Dublin, but they moved to France a few years ago."

"What makes you think he went out for a run this morning?" Walsh asks.

"He runs every day. He's training for a marathon. Also, his running shoes are gone."

Walsh coughs into his fist and regards me with an apologetic air. "And you didn't have a falling out or anything of that nature?"

I eye him indignantly. "We're here on our honeymoon."

"Right." Walsh consults his notebook. "Would you have any reason to think he might want to harm himself?"

"Absolutely not! Like I told you already, we're newlyweds."

"I'm obliged to ask," Walsh responds, looking somewhat sheepish. "The cliffs have a bit of a reputation, if you know what I mean."

I don't, but I can hazard a guess. I shoot an anguished

look at Moira who's hovering in the background, brewing a fresh pot of tea.

"Sure isn't it clear the poor man's lost?" she says briskly, carrying a tray of tea and cookies over to us. "Can you get a search party out this late in the day?"

Walsh rumples his brow. "We'll go door-to-door and make enquiries, but it'll be morning before we can get a missing persons' search sorted. We'll need to call in a dog unit from Ennis."

I blink uncomprehendingly at him. "How far away is that?"

"Thirty minutes," Doyle interjects.

I thread my fingers distractedly through my hair. We're moving at a snail's pace. It will be dark if they don't start looking for Declan soon. The thought of him spending the night exposed to the elements fills me with dread. "What about a helicopter?" I ask.

"Not in this weather. We'll contact the Coast Guard first thing in the morning," Walsh assures me. "Do you mind if I have a look through your husband's belongings?"

I give a disheartened shrug and get to my feet. "Anything to help." I lead him into the bedroom, my cheeks flushing when I survey the trail of abandoned clothing, empty champagne bottle, and unmade bed. "I ... haven't had a chance to tidy up, yet."

Garda Walsh points to Declan's sweatshirt hanging on the back of a chair. "Would you mind if we take that with us? We'll need an article of clothing for the dogs."

A shiver runs across my shoulders. "Take whatever you need," I reply, reaching for Declan's Dallas Cowboys sweatshirt and handing it over.

Walsh sticks his head into the ensuite bathroom. "Is your husband on any life-saving medication?"

"No, he's in perfect health. He's an athlete."

"Whose phone is that?" Walsh gestures to the iPhone plugged into the wall by the bed.

"Declan's. He doesn't take it with him when he runs."

"Have you checked his messages and emails?" Walsh asks.

"What for? He would call my phone if he was trying to get in touch."

"Maybe he arranged to meet up with somebody."

I quickly unplug the phone, too embarrassed to admit the thought hadn't even occurred to me. After punching in the code—my birthday—I scroll through Declan's messages. There are a couple from Brynn, wondering how he's enjoying Ireland so far, begging for pictures. I cringe at the growing realization that I'll have to respond to her soon or she'll begin to worry. I'll either have to break the news to her that her father is missing or send a message pretending to be Declan—staving off the inevitable in the hope that he shows up. Both options fill me with dread. I scan through his emails but there's nothing to indicate he was planning on meeting anyone.

"Anything?" Walsh prompts.

I shake my head. "We deliberately didn't make any plans for our stay. We wanted to be spontaneous."

Garda Walsh nods. "I'll need to take your husband's phone with me. Forensics might find something on it."

I grimace. Declan's not going to be happy if he arrives back and finds his phone gone. But the last thing I want to do is appear uncooperative. As far as Walsh is concerned, I'm a potential person of interest in my husband's disappearance. I don't know the protocol when it comes to missing persons' investigations in Ireland, but I know I need the gardaí on my side. I have no one else. Reluctantly, I hand over the phone.

Walsh fixes a steely gaze on me. "I'll need your passports too."

This time I don't ask why. He's making sure I can't leave the country.

5

_____

After the police leave, it takes me another half hour or so to persuade Moira to go home. I appreciate her kindness, but she's been fussing around me like a mother hen, and I really need to be alone so I can think. Despite wanting her to leave, it's a little eerie in the cottage without her motherly presence. I'm now faced with the unsettling prospect of spending the second night of my honeymoon here alone. A staccato rapping on the window almost makes me jump out of my skin. I leap up, convinced someone is trying to get my attention. I don't see anyone outside, but it leaves me on edge, nonetheless.

I'm torn about whether I should call Brynn now or wait until morning. By then, I might have some real news—good or bad. There's no point in alarming her until I know for sure it's unavoidable. After mulling things over, I decide to call Maddie instead, and check in with work. I won't mention anything about Declan being missing—not until I have to. It will be all over the office in half a second and I don't want to deal with the deluge of cloaked-in-concern prying texts that will inevitably follow. I dial Maddie's direct line, but the call goes straight to voicemail. I try the receptionist next and ask her to locate my assistant for me. "I'm sorry, Abby," she replies in her usual maddening chirp. "Maddie's not in today. She called in sick the morning of your wedding."

My stomach twists at the news. The timing couldn't be worse. I left a lot of important work for her to handle in my absence—an absence that might turn out to be longer than I anticipated. "Any idea when she'll be back?"

"Hard to say. She has the flu," the receptionist replies. "All depends how she feels, I suppose."

I hang up and sink back into the couch. My stress level has ratcheted up another few notches. I was confident in Maddie's ability to manage my projects on my behalf, but knowing they'll be piling up in my absence gives me one more thing to worry about just when I need it least.

My phone rings and I frown at the unfamiliar number on the screen. "Hello?" I say, pressing the speaker button to take the call.

"Abby, this is Garda Walsh. I wanted to ask if you'd be okay with me passing Declan's photo along to the media. RTÉ, one of our TV stations, is wanting to cover the search and rescue efforts tomorrow. It would be good to have them involved. The more people who see Declan's face, the quicker he'll be found."

I blink to trap the scalding tears threatening to spill down my cheeks. The thought of seeing Declan's face plastered on Irish television makes this nightmare all too real. My husband of two days has vanished without a trace in a foreign country—granted, a westernized country that speaks English, but I'm still five-thousand miles from home. I feel so alone and utterly helpless. I'm used to taking charge and having everything under control. I don't do well with unknown variables. I'm a controller, after all. "Yes ... of course. That's fine," I manage to choke out.

"Very good," Walsh says. "You'll be hearing from me in the morning as soon as I have an update on the search efforts."

I curl up on the couch, clutching my phone in disbelief that this is happening. *Where are you, Declan? Are you hurt, lost ... dead?*

Maybe it's sheer exhaustion, or perhaps it's the sound of the rain splashing off the windowsill, but I can't hold back the tears anymore. I bury my face in a cushion and sob until my entire body aches. Declan and I should be curled up on this couch together right now, enjoying the crackling flames of a warm fire, listening to the splatter of the rain outside, making plans for tomorrow, and the next day, and the rest of our lives. Declan was the second chance I thought I'd never get, a caring, compassionate man who isn't afraid to show his tender side. When my dog Aspen passed away unexpectedly a few months after we met, he even ordered a custom casket for her and helped me bury her in the backyard. An ugly sob sticks in my throat at the memory. We talked about adopting a shelter dog after the honeymoon. I don't know if that will ever happen now. My entire life feels like it's crashing down around me all over again.

When I finally manage to compose myself, I reach for my phone and draft a text to Brynn. I rewrite and delete it at least a dozen times before I hit send.

My battery's dead. Pictures coming soon. Dad xoxo

If they don't find Declan by tomorrow, I'll tell her the truth. Until then, there's no sense in both of us facing the prospect of a sleepless night.

. . .

When I wake the following morning, the first thing that strikes me is that the rain has stopped. I roll over in bed to nudge Declan and ask him if he wants to go on a hike. Then, it all comes rushing back and the horror of the situation hits me like a tornado. I wrap my arms around myself, not wanting to accept it, or even to get out of bed and face the day. Declan hasn't found his way back to the cottage during the night, which is a clear indication that he's injured or unconscious—or worse.

Wearily, I crawl out from beneath the covers and make my way to the kitchen. Moira has left me well stocked with food, but even the sight of her homemade scones turns my insides to mush. I make myself a strong cup of coffee and turn on the television. I scroll through several channels, some of them in Gaelic, before finding RTÉ. The newscaster and a guest commentator are discussing renewable gas options to de-carbonize rural Ireland. I zone in and out, catching something about an upcoming teachers' strike before the scene switches to an outdoor setting. My eyes snap to the screen when I realize the reporter clutching a microphone on a windy cliff top is talking about a missing tourist. I scoot to the edge of the couch and turn up the volume as she begins to speak. "Fears heightened today for the safety of an American tourist who went missing yesterday in County Clare. Declan Cafferty from Los Angeles, California, disappeared after going out for an early morning run. Gardaí confirm they are becoming increasingly concerned for his welfare."

A photo of Declan fills the screen and I press my knuckles to my lips. *This can't be happening—not to us, not on our honeymoon.*

The camera pans to a group of assembled search and rescue volunteers in neon orange vests. "The Coast Guard has deployed a helicopter, and ground searches are being conducted in the area," the reporter continues. "Volunteers are also using drones with thermal imaging capability in an effort to locate the missing man."

A number to call with any information comes up on the screen. Moments later, the newscaster moves on to the weather forecast, and, just like that, Declan Cafferty is forgotten by everyone but me.

I cover my face with my hands and take a few deep breaths as I contemplate my next steps. It won't be long before the story's all over social media, and I can't risk Brynn finding out from strangers that her father is missing. It's the middle of the night in Los Angeles, but she's a night owl. There's a chance she might be texting or gaming with her friends. I can't put this off any longer.

Swallowing down a burgeoning ball of dread, I reach for my phone and dial Brynn's number. It rings and rings before going to voicemail. I close my eyes and take a steadying breath, then try the number again.

"Hello," a sleepy voice answers.

"Brynn, it's Abby."

"Oh, hi. I thought I was dreaming when my phone rang. How's Ireland?" She yawns loudly, barely skipping a beat before breezing on. "Is it as beautiful as everyone says? I texted Dad to hurry up and send some pictures, but Aunt Jamie says not to bug him on his honeymoon. My friend's cousin went to—"

"Brynn! Listen to me, please," I cut in.

For a moment there's silence and then she speaks again, her voice subdued this time. "What is it? What's wrong?"

"It's your dad. He went running yesterday and he hasn't come back, yet."

"What? Why didn't you tell me this yesterday? Wait! He texted me. He must—"

"That was me, Brynn. I didn't want to worry you. I was hoping he'd simply got lost or something. It was raining heavily so it would have been easy to take a wrong turn on these country roads."

"Are you saying Dad's been out all night in the rain?" Brynn asks, sounding aghast.

"We ... don't know that for sure."

"We? Who's we?"

"The police are looking for him. Search and rescue volunteers too. I'm sure they'll find him soon. They've deployed drones, and a dog unit, even a Coast Guard helicopter."

"The *Coast* Guard," Brynn repeats, enunciating the words as though they're contraband. "Do they think he's been swept out to sea or something?"

"No! Not at all," I lie. "Sometimes it's easier to spot someone from a helicopter. You can scout places that are hard to get to on foot."

"I want to come over there. I want to help," Brynn says, in a faltering tone.

I wince at the pain in her voice. "I know you do, honey, but it's too early for that. There's a good chance the police will find your dad in the next few hours. He might have just twisted an ankle. It doesn't make sense for you to take off school and fly all the way over here."

"I'm scared," Brynn wails. "It feels like it's happening all over again. First Mom, and now Dad."

I scrunch my eyes shut, searching for the right words to comfort her. I know that sickening feeling only too well— that history is repeating itself. Why does bad stuff have to happen to people who've already suffered a heart-wrenching loss? I bring a shaky hand to my forehead, trying to clear my thoughts. I have to shelve my own needs, for now, and focus on Brynn. I made that commitment to her and Declan only a couple of days ago, and now I have my first real opportunity to prove I meant it.

"I know you're scared, Brynn, but try to be brave just a little longer. Think positively. He can't have gone far. They showed his picture on the news—everyone is looking for him. I know we're going to find him soon."

I swallow the hard lump in my throat when I end the call promising to keep her updated throughout the day.

I do believe we'll find Declan, but will he be dead or alive?

6

Garda Walsh introduces me to several members of the search and rescue team who have stopped by the folding tables where I'm helping hand out cups of tea and sandwiches donated by some of the locals. I couldn't sit in the cottage chewing my fingers ragged for another minute, hoping for an update. An RTÉ news reporter came by the tables earlier and interviewed me. The story has really taken off—there are dozens of locals here, offering to help with the search, hungry for more details. Everyone's intrigued by the romantic suspense element—a husband disappearing on his honeymoon has all the makings of a sensational movie. *Second chance romance gone wrong*, a local radio station has dubbed it.

The working theory is that Declan injured himself while running and either slipped into a ravine or down a cliff. Despite the search efforts centering around the coast, I'm well aware the gardaí are keeping a close eye on me as well. Walsh has an aura of disarming friendliness that belies his astute mind. He questioned me again this morning about my movements the morning Declan disappeared, and our passports still haven't been returned to me. Not that it matters. I have no plans to leave the country, and I'm fully cooperating with every request. The authorities can question me all they want. I have nothing to hide, and I had nothing to do with Declan's disappearance. The constant rehashing of questions is more frustrating than anything else, knowing the police are wasting precious time and resources interrogating me. Still, I'm putting my faith in them finding Declan. They're all I have.

It's only when I'm tidying up the tables after lunch that I discover a note folded in quarters, tucked beneath one of the sandwich platters. It looks like a page torn from a notebook with my first name scrawled on top in childlike handwriting. My chest tightens. It's more than likely a note of sympathy from a reticent well-wisher, but there's always a chance someone has information on Declan's whereabouts. I unfold it with trembling fingers and read what's inside.

Shane knows.

I stare at the words, trying to make sense of them. Knows *what* exactly? I rumple my brow, shuffling through several possibilities in my head. Does he know where Declan is? Or what happened to him? Maybe he saw something. Or does it mean Shane is somehow involved in my husband's disappearance? The dreadful thought hangs there as my brain tries to make sense of it. Thinking back on it, it struck me as odd when he told me there was no need to call the police. Whatever the case, I need to find Walsh ASAP and show him the note. I abandon the cleanup to the other women bustling around the tables and step aside to make a call. "Someone left me a note," I blurt out the second Walsh answers. "I think it might be important."

"What does it say?"

"Just two words. *Shane knows*. He must have seen something."

"Who gave it to you?" Walsh asks.

"No one. It was left anonymously under a sandwich platter, addressed to me."

Walsh mumbles a grunt of acknowledgement. "Hold on to it, for now. I'm on my way."

"Aren't you going to question Shane?"

"I will, once I have the note in hand," Walsh replies. "I want to see his reaction to it."

"I'll go with you," I say.

FORTY MINUTES LATER, Walsh and I pull up outside the Murphys' farmhouse.

"Let me do the talking," Walsh cautions. "I don't want Shane on the back foot and clamming up on us. He's not a big talker at the best of times, as you might have gathered by now."

I turn to look directly at Walsh, almost afraid to ask. "You … don't think Shane might have done something to Declan, do you?"

Walsh gives an emphatic shake of his head. "No. He wouldn't hurt a fly. There's a good chance the note is just someone taking a hand at him. He's an easy target. A bit slow, if you know what I mean."

"I see," I say, keeping my thoughts to myself. I don't know if I agree with the general consensus on Shane. His morbid stare unnerves me, but then I don't know him as well as the locals do. Maybe he's not deliberately trying to intimidate me.

"Has Shane ever been in trouble with the law?" I ask, as I exit the car.

Garda Walsh throws me a circumspect look. "Ah now, you have nothing to worry about. Like I said before, the lad's harmless. Maybe he knows something and maybe he doesn't. Either way, we'll get to the bottom of it."

I nod, trying to ignore the relentless parade of unsettling thoughts marching through my mind.

Moira answers the door and shows us into the sitting room, gesturing for us to take a seat on a faded, chintz-upholstered sofa. She angles her face toward me. "Any news?"

I clasp my hands tightly in my lap. "Not yet."

"Could I have a word with your Shane if he's home?" Walsh asks.

Moira puts a hand on her hip. "Whatever for?"

"We're interviewing all the locals," Walsh explains. "It's possible Shane might have seen something and not realized the significance of it."

Moira gives a mollified nod. "Aye, he wouldn't know what he saw, would he? I'll get him for you." She yells up the stairs before disappearing into the kitchen to make us the ubiquitous cup of tea.

Moments later, I hear a series of heavy thuds as Shane descends the stairs like a reluctant child dragging his heels. He stands in the doorway staring solemnly at me. I squirm in my seat under his unrelenting gaze until Moira bustles up behind him carrying a laden tray and elbows him into the room. He plonks down on a chair in the far corner and stuffs his hands into his pockets.

Before Garda Walsh has a chance to ask him anything, he leans forward in his chair and addresses me, "S-s-some honeymoon, eh?"

I stiffen. It's an exact repeat of what he said to me in the car yesterday. I can't quite put my finger on his tone. Is it a question? Is he being sarcastic, or is he sympathizing with me? Does he secretly relish the fact that my honeymoon has been an unmitigated disaster so far? If he had something to do with Declan's disappearance, he might be getting some kind of twisted satisfaction from watching me suffer. A chill snakes down my shoulders. He always seems to have eyes on me. I can't help thinking back to the tapping sound on my window last night. Shane strikes me as the type to go around peeking in windows. I hope he hasn't been down at the cottage trying to freak me out now that I'm alone.

Garda Walsh accepts a cup of tea from Moira and clears his throat. "Shane, did you happen to see Declan Cafferty out running yesterday?"

An uneasy look flits across his face before his eyes swivel in my direction.

"Shane!" Moira snaps. "Answer the garda's question!"

He drops his gaze to the floor, his knee bouncing up and down. "N-n-no."

"Are you sure about that?" Walsh presses. "You're not in any kind of trouble, Shane. We're just trying to find the man."

Shane shoots a suspicious look at me.

"I just want to find my husband," I say softly. "If you saw anything, or know anything, I would be really grateful if you could tell us."

"Think, Shane!" Moira admonishes him. "Get your hands out of your pockets and answer the lady."

I recoil inwardly at the way she talks to her adult son. Then again, he seems content to play the part of an over-grown child. Despite his stutter, I can't imagine he isn't capable of more than she gives him credit for. He had no problem driving my rental car, although judging by Walsh's reaction, I suspect he doesn't have a driver's license.

Shane pulls one hand out of his pocket and places it on his knee in an effort to stop it from jerking up and down. "I did-didn't s-s-see him."

"Do you know where he is?" Walsh prompts.

Shane furrows his brow before hiding his face with his arm and shaking his head.

Garda Walsh rubs a hand over his jaw. "The thing is, Shane, someone seems to think you know something about Declan's disappearance."

Moira narrows her eyes. "And who would that be? Enid McNally sticking her nose in where it doesn't belong?"

"It's none of your neighbors, Moira," Walsh assures her. "Just an anonymous tip—a note in fact." He pulls it out of his pocket and flattens it on the coffee table in front of Shane. "*Shane knows,*" Walsh reads. "What do you think that means?"

Shane's eyes flicker with fear. He folds his arms in front of him and tucks his chin into his chest, rocking gently back and forth.

Moira sets down her cup with a clatter. "It'll just be some eejits acting the maggot—messing with him again. You're wasting your time."

Garda Walsh appraises Shane for a long moment and then slaps his thighs. "All right. We'll be off then. If you think of anything at all that might be helpful, please ring the station right away."

Moira escorts us to the door and pats me on the arm. "I'll bring you down some dinner later."

"Thank you," I say, not wanting to appear rude, even though I'm sure I won't be able to eat a bite.

Walsh and I ride in silence back down the lane to the cottage. My brain feels like there's a damp fog moving in, rusting the gears.

"That wasn't very productive," Walsh says, when he pulls up to the front door. "I had a feeling it wouldn't amount to much. It's not the first time Shane's been at the receiving end of a practical joke."

"If the note's a joke, it's in very poor taste, considering the circumstances," I say, as I reach for my purse.

"That it is, and I can only extend my apologies on behalf of any youngsters behind it."

I give a forlorn nod. "Any updates from the search party?"

"Nothing yet," Walsh answers, glancing at his phone. "I'll be sure to ring you if there are any developments going into the evening."

My phone pings with an incoming message and I glance distractedly at the screen, hoping it isn't Brynn again.

Terror rips through my veins when I read the words.

We have your husband.

7

Walsh quirks a questioning brow. "What is it? Have you heard from Declan?"

I reread the message on my phone, my emotions spinning like batter in a mixing bowl as I try to decipher it. Has Declan been found? Or does this mean something else entirely? Dread curls in my stomach. What if the note harbors some sinister meaning?

"I ... got a message but I'm not sure who it's from," I stammer. "It says, *we have your husband.* Do you think search and rescue has found him?" My gaze locks on Garda Walsh. I don't trust myself to interpret the message correctly. There are too many nuances to the way the Irish wield their words. Maybe I'm missing something.

Walsh's grip on the steering wheel tightens. For the first time since we met, he looks perturbed. I know before he answers that I'm not going to like what he has to say. "Search and rescue would have got in touch with me if they'd found him. Can I take a look at that message?"

With a mounting sense of dread, I pass him my phone.

He studies the screen, his forehead creasing. "Is this the only message you got?"

"Yes." I chew on my lip. "Should I respond?"

Garda Walsh gives a somber nod. "Ask them who this is and where Declan is."

My finger shakes as I tap out a text.

Time seems to move at an achingly slow pace before a response pops up on the screen.

No questions. Follow directions.

Walsh and I read the message together in silence. My heart hammers beneath my ribs. I can almost hear the sound of it echoing off the paneling in the car. There's no denying the menacing undertone to the second text. "What does it mean?" I rasp. "It sounds like a threat—like Declan's been abducted."

"We'll treat it as such for now," Walsh responds, his face a mask of practiced calm. "There's a possibility it's only pranksters injecting themselves into the situation. We'll put a trace on the phone, but they could be using a prepaid."

I squeeze my sweating hands together in my lap, scarcely able to grasp what he's saying. This is all so unbelievable. How can it be happening? I know it's not a dream, but maybe it's a sick joke. Maybe I'm on one of those hidden camera shows. The Irish are known to be big pranksters. Would Declan willingly have gone along with something like this? I'm tempted to ask Walsh if he's in on some hilarious honeymoon gag, but something in his expression tells me his concern is real. "Who would have abducted him?" I ask. "And why? They couldn't have pegged him for a rich tourist while he was out running with no camera, and no wallet."

Walsh grimaces as his radio crackles to life. "No sense speculating. We'll have to wait on a message with directions.

In the meantime, can you check and see if any money has been withdrawn from your bank accounts?"

I flash him a startled look. "Do you think someone might be holding him for ransom?"

"Could be." Walsh rubs a hand over the nape of his neck. "They might try and force him to make a withdrawal. We need to keep an open mind at this point."

He turns his attention to his radio and barks out a series of orders, slipping into an accent so thick I can't make out half of what he's saying.

A beep in my lap indicates another message. I pick up my phone and read it, blood draining from my head.

Follow these instructions if you want to see your husband alive again!

1. Do not contact the police or any other authorities or private parties.

2. Put 1 million euro in small, unmarked bills in a suitcase and take it to 32 Cronan Road, Ballinakill within 72 hours. NO EXCUSES! NO EXCEPTIONS!

3. Leave the suitcase on the back steps then text this number for the address where your husband is being held.

Someone will be watching you at all times. DO NOT DEVIATE from these instructions or your husband will die!

When Walsh is done talking, I pass him my phone. As he reads the message, his expression darkens.

"Right," he says, starting up the car. "Time to set up a task force."

Ten minutes later, we pull up outside the local Garda station—a two-story former residence with gray, peeling plaster walls and stacked chimneys. Inside, it's a hive of activity and I suddenly feel completely overwhelmed by the situation. Everything is unfamiliar, and despite the kindness of the officers who ply me with endless cups of tea and soothing words, fear is eating me up inside. If Declan has been abducted, his life's in real danger. The statistics are sobering—I'm only too aware that not all abductions have happy endings.

A female police officer with sky-blue eyes and thick, dark hair coiled into a tight bun approaches me in her sensible heels. "Mrs. Cafferty, if you'd like to come with me, I'll get you sorted with a computer." She leads me into a stuffy office and pulls out a swivel chair with a burst seam for me to sit on. After showing me how to log on to the internet, she takes my phone for a forensics exam and leaves me to pull up our bank accounts. I log into Declan's personal account first. The last transaction was made the day of our wedding. He withdrew five-hundred dollars that morning—cash for our honeymoon, largely unspent.

I move on to our joint account next but there's no suspicious activity, or in my personal account. I roll my knotted shoulders as I stare at the considerable balance. The settlement from the sale of my first husband's business came through two months ago. I'd been tangled up in court with his former business partner ever since Eric's death, and it was a relief to finally close the door on that chapter of my life. After paying the lawyers, I ended up clearing a little over 1.3 million dollars. Eric's partner walked away with a lot more, but I was just glad to be done with the lawsuit. I haven't touched the money, yet. Declan and I talked about investing it in rental properties, but it wasn't something we wanted to rush into before the wedding. My finger hovers over the logout button. I have enough money to pay the ransom, but could I get that amount wired to Ireland in seventy-two hours?

There's a rap on the door and I jerk my head up as Garda Walsh strides into the room. "We're still working on assembling the task force, but forensics has confirmed that whoever's texting you is using a prepaid phone." He gestures to the computer. "Have you had a chance to check your bank accounts?"

"Yes. Nothing's been touched." I hesitate before adding, "I don't know what the protocol is in these situations. Should I go ahead and agree to pay the ransom? I don't want to play games with my husband's life."

Walsh blinks, looking momentarily taken aback. "Are you saying you'd be able to get your hands on that kind of money?"

I sigh and lean back in the uncomfortable chair, picking distractedly at the exposed foam. "I received a settlement from my first husband's business recently. The case has been tied up in court for years."

Walsh frowns. "How recently?"

"A couple of months before the wedding."

His jaw hardens. "And your new husband—Declan—does he know about this money?"

I fire him an indignant look, not liking the direction the conversation is taking. "Of course. What are you insinuating?"

He exhales a heavy breath. "Nothing, yet, but we need to take every angle into consideration. Let me talk to the task force about how best to proceed with the ransom demand."

He turns and exits the room before I can respond.

I sit in shocked silence for several minutes, weighing his line of questioning. It's ridiculous to think Declan might be involved in anything so egregious. I shouldn't have mentioned the settlement money. If the police suspect Declan staged his own abduction, it will detract from the urgency of the situation. They might even call off search and rescue efforts. It makes no sense to suspect Declan of trying to extort money from me. Why would he? He's married to me, and I didn't make him sign a prenup. My money is his money as far as I'm concerned. Besides, he didn't know about the money when we met, and it was never guaranteed as long as the case was tied up in court.

Anger simmers in my gut as I contemplate just how outrageous the whole idea of Declan swindling me out of my money is. His life's in danger and that's what the police should be focusing on. Brynn's face flashes to mind and my throat tightens. I promised to love and protect her, as well as her dad. I have no choice but to pay that ransom.

Before I can second-guess myself, I pick up the phone on the desk and place an international call to my bank in Los Angeles.

8

—————

It's clear from his expression Garda Walsh is not happy with what I've done, but he tells me the task force will stand by my decision and oversee the logistics of delivering the ransom. "But before you hand over the money, you need to ask for proof that they have your husband." He clears his throat before adding, "And ... that he's alive."

I give a mute nod. "Forensics still has my phone."

Walsh exits the room and returns a few minutes later with a plastic evidence bag. I pull out my phone and read through the ransom instructions again before typing out a response.

I'll get you the money. I need proof you have my husband.

I show it to Walsh and he nods approvingly. "Let me know as soon as they get back to you. I need to step out to make a quick call."

Five minutes go by, and then ten, and just when I've convinced myself the ransom message was a hoax—like the stupid note about Shane—an image pops into my messages.

I click on it and immediately clap my hand to my mouth in shock. It's Declan sitting on a dirt floor looking stoically at the camera, arms bound behind his back. I stifle a moan, appalled at his bedraggled appearance and what appears to be bruising on one side of his face. "Walsh!" I call out.

He strides back into the room and peers at the screen in my hand, his brows twitching toward one another.

"Why did they have to hurt him?" I whimper. "I told them I'd give them the money."

"They might have tried to get it from him first and he refused to cooperate," Walsh replies grimly. "Rest assured, we'll do everything we can to bring your husband home safely."

I BARELY SLEEP for the next two nights. I spend most of the time hunkered down in the Airbnb while Walsh sends me updates on the task force's progress. Other than handing out flyers, or walking around town and along the beach asking strangers if they've seen my husband, there's precious little I can do until the money from my US bank account comes through. I've been avoiding checking in with work—I'm just not up to fending off questions I don't have answers to. The only person I can really pour my heart out to is my best friend, Kelly—Kells, as I affectionately call her—but until I get back to Los Angeles, all she can do is offer her thoughts and prayers and urge me not to give up hope. I try to keep Brynn updated on events as they unfold but, naturally, she's beside herself with worry, and her tone grows increasingly antagonistic each time we talk. It feels like rejection when I'm in so much pain myself, but I understand that she has no one to take her frustration out on other than me. She's stuck on the other side of the Atlantic relying on me to make this right.

She hasn't gone to school for the past few days, and her Aunt Jamie, whom she's staying with, had to take a few days off work to keep an eye on her. I don't think Brynn would do anything impulsive—like try and book a flight to Ireland—but it's hard to know with teenagers. At sixteen, I doubt she'd be allowed to travel alone on an international flight anyway.

So far, the police haven't been able to identify Declan's kidnappers, and no group has claimed responsibility. Walsh assures me the days of terrorists abducting people are gone, so that's some small comfort. The ransom money has been wired from my account in Los Angeles to a local bank, but the seventy-two-hour deadline is fast approaching, and the money still hasn't come through. The task force has instructed me to wait until the final hour and then text Declan's kidnappers to assure them the money is coming and request an extension. I hope it doesn't come down to that. Relying on the goodwill of kidnappers with a penchant for violence doesn't give me a warm and cozy feeling. There's a good chance they'll take it out on Declan if I fail to comply with their deadline.

When the call finally comes from the local bank that my money has arrived, I'm weak with relief at the thought of this nightmare coming to a close. Everything moves quickly after that. Walsh deploys officers to stake out the deserted farmhouse where I've been told to take the suitcase filled with money. I can barely breathe at the thought of seeing Declan again. I hope he's all right. It's hard to tell the extent of his injuries from the photo. Walsh has an ambulance on standby to take him straight to the hospital to get him checked out, which gives me some peace of mind.

As instructed, I drive my rental car to the bank alone. The ransom message said someone would be watching me and I can't help eying everyone on the road with an air of suspicion as they go about their business—any one of them could be working with the kidnappers. When I reach the coastal town of LaHinch, where the bank is located, the manager whisks me into his office and a clerk helps me fill the suitcase under the watchful eye of an undercover member of the task force.

"When you reach the farmhouse, go straight to the back door and deposit the suitcase," the officer instructs me. "Don't knock, don't call out, and don't look around for anyone. Walk slowly back to your car and wait for a text from the kidnappers with Declan's location. As soon as it comes through, forward it to Walsh. He'll meet you there. Under no circumstances are you to attempt to retrieve your husband until backup arrives. We'll clear the site and bring him out to you. Any questions?"

I tug at my sleeve nervously. "What if the kidnappers don't text me an address afterward?"

"There's no reason to believe they won't," the officer reassures me, with a tight smile that doesn't quite reach his eyes. "Once they have their money, they'll be eager to unload their hostage. We won't move in on them until your husband's safe."

The farmhouse where I've been instructed to make the drop is a little over twenty kilometers out of town. The road seems to grow darker and narrower the farther I drive. Each time I spot a vehicle in my rearview mirror, I worry it might be someone tailing me, but the minute they get a clear line of sight they pull out and zip right by. Maybe it was just an idle threat on the kidnappers' part.

My hand sweats profusely as I grip the gearshift. Only a

little while longer, and Declan will be safe. I picture us calling Brynn together and telling her the good news. The nightmare is almost over. Declan will soon be free. I repeat these mantras to myself as I drive. I have to believe the drop will go off without a hitch. Declan and I picked Ireland for our honeymoon because it's always been a dream of mine to visit here. Staying in a stone cottage on a farm near the ocean sounded hopelessly romantic. Never in my wildest dreams did I think I would end up negotiating with kidnappers for my husband's life.

As I turn onto the dirt lane that leads to the isolated farmhouse, my chest tightens. The rutted lane is overgrown with weeds, and the VW Golf creaks in protest as it bumps in and out of waterlogged potholes—making me thankful we caved and bought the overpriced damage waiver from the rental agency. At the rate I'm going, I'll have maxed it out by the time I return the vehicle. As I drive, I nervously scan the fields framed with stacked, lichen-covered stone walls. There's not another soul in sight. Other than a few black-and-white cows munching robotically on a distant hill, I can't see another living being. But I know I'm not alone. Walsh promised me the task force would be in position before I got here. If things go awry, I can count on them coming to my rescue. I only hope they get to Declan in time.

Moments later, a derelict, gable-ended farmhouse comes into view. Several of the windows are boarded up and the walls are thickly infested with ivy. The flagstone path leading up to the front door has long since disappeared beneath a jungle of weeds. I check the time before slipping my phone into my coat pocket—I'm still within the deadline, barely. When I step out of the car, I don't detect any sign of company, good or bad. I'm about to reach for the suitcase on the back seat when my phone buzzes with another message from the kidnappers.

Drop's off. You compromised the location. We told you we would be watching.

9

———

I dart a panic-stricken glance around me. Where are the kidnappers? And how do they know the police are here? Maybe they're watching me through binoculars. My chilled skin prickles as I tap on my phone and quickly type out a response.

I don't understand. I have the money.

Five relentless minutes go by, fear tripping switches in my brain, before I receive a response.

Leave the money inside the ruins at this pinned location. Empty out the suitcase and take it with you. DO IT NOW AND DO NOT CONTACT THE POLICE OR HE DIES! Text us when the drop's been made.

Terror-stricken, I get back inside the car and turn on the ignition. I blink back the tears threatening to blind me as I click on the pinned location and load the directions. I feel the eerie presence of eyes on me, but I can't tell if it's the officers staking out the farmhouse, or the kidnappers. Goosebumps travel up and down my arms as I put the car in gear. The thought that I've enraged the thugs who have my husband chills my soul. They threatened Declan's life, but they've given me a second chance. I can't risk involving the police again. I have no choice but to take the money to the new location and pray they release my husband unharmed.

I turn the rental car around in the muddy yard and crawl back down the rutted lane. I briefly consider dialing Walsh's number, but I can't bring myself to gamble with Declan's life. Before I reach the main road, my phone pings with another message. I change gears and slow down to read it. This time the kidnappers have sent a video. I click on it, and suck in a sharp breath at the sight of Declan lying on the floor, unmoving, one eye swollen shut. His bottom lip is split, and there's a patch of what appears to be dried blood on his cheek. From the right side of the screen a black boot kicks him in the ribs and he moans softly. The message below the video reads: *he's alive ... for now.*

I choke out a strangled sob. I can barely breathe at the sight of my husband writhing in pain. The kidnappers are making sure I understand what's at stake. I betrayed them once, but they won't overlook a second infraction. I step on the gas, no longer caring what the potholes are doing to the car's suspension. All I can think about is ending Declan's suffering at the hands of these maniacs. When I reach the main road, I follow the GPS directions, driving as fast as I dare on these treacherous roads. Walsh keeps calling, but I ignore him. I check my rearview mirror, discomfited at the presence of a white Mercedes van keeping its distance behind me. For once, the vehicle makes no attempt to pass. I have a disconcerting feeling it's the kidnappers making sure I follow their instructions this time.

I turn onto an overgrown lane and follow it for a quarter mile or so until I see the looming shadow of a partly demolished stone tower up ahead. When my GPS confirms that I've arrived, I park next to a cattle gate and sit quietly for a moment, surveying the scene. The white van hasn't followed me up the lane, and I don't detect any movement in the area, but odds are someone is watching me. And this time no one's coming to my rescue if things go awry.

My pulse pounds in my throat as I climb out into the bracing wind. I haul the suitcase out of the car for a second time, half-expecting to feel a bullet hit me in the back. It would be an easy task to dispose of me at this deserted location. I try wheeling the case across the field toward the ruin, but it's far too bumpy. Abandoning the attempt, I lift it instead and set out for the tower, my gaze zigzagging in all directions. The case grows heavier with every step and my breath seems to be scraping up my throat as I edge closer to the shadowy tower. I wonder if this is where the kidnappers will make the exchange, or if I'll have to drive to yet another location to retrieve Declan. The thought of seeing him again gives me a much-needed jolt of adrenalin and I duck my head into the wind and continue plodding up the hill.

When I finally reach the ruin, I throw a cautious glance around the area before stepping inside. What's left of the stone tower is heavily graffitied and the ground is littered with beer cans. There's no sign of Declan, nor any indication he was ever here. I hurriedly dump the contents of the suitcase out and then turn and jog back down to the car, trying not to twist my ankle in the process. I clamber back behind the wheel and send the kidnappers a message confirming the drop. Their response comes through almost immediately.

Drive back to the bank. Tell the manager the plan has changed and you are to wire the money to account #CIMGKYKY3983614883 one hour after your arrival. DO NOT tell them the suitcase is empty before the hour is up or HE DIES!

DO NOT alert the police. If you follow these instructions precisely we will send your husband's location.

Sweat dots my forehead as I plug in the directions for the return trip to the town of LaHinch. I don't know if I can make it through an hour of waiting at the bank without blurting out the truth—this will be the most agonizing sixty minutes of my life. When I pull into the parking lot, I take a moment to compose myself before going back inside. The bank manager's eyes widen when he sees me. He pats his flushed face with a handkerchief. "What are you doing here?" he asks, his gaze darting anxiously between me and the suitcase as he ushers me back to his office.

"They called off the drop," I explain. "They must have known there were officers staked out around the farmhouse. They told me to wire them the money one hour from now instead."

The manager huffs out a heavy breath, smoothing a hand over his bald head. "I don't like the sound of this. Have you notified the gardaí?"

"The kidnappers warned me not to, or they'll kill Declan. I'll call the gardaí as soon as the transfer goes through, but I can't jeopardize the deal and risk my husband's life."

"Very well," the manager agrees with a reluctant sigh. "What's the account number?"

I read it off to him and he frowns in concentration. "Caymen Islands. The account will be hard to trace." He gestures to the suitcase. "Let me have the money and I'll set up the transfer."

"No!" I tighten my grip on the handle of the suitcase. "I'm not allowed to turn it over until the hour is up. They were very specific about that."

The bank manager rubs an agitated hand over the back of his neck. "Fine. We'll do it their way."

A bank clerk brings me a cup of tea and I take a welcome sip of the strong brew, savoring the warmth. I close my eyes briefly, picturing Declan's battered face once more. Was this really a random kidnapping? Did someone watch him leave the Airbnb and try to shake him down for money? The strange note about Shane knowing something bothers me. I can't rid myself of the notion that he might have had something to do with Declan's abduction. Moira dismissed the note as a prank, but I noticed how Shane's eyes widened at the sight of it. Did he tip someone off that Americans were staying in the Airbnb? But how would they have known we had money? I suppose they could have beaten it out of Declan. No one could be expected to withstand that kind of abuse.

An hour later, the bank manager comes back into the office, tugging at his tie. "Are you ready to make the transfer?"

I double check the time, then kneel down and open the suitcase, laying it flat on the ground. "I'm sorry I had to lie to you. The kidnappers made me drop the money off at a new location. The transfer story was to buy them some time."

The color seeps from the bank manager's face. "You'd better notify the gardaí right away before the kidnappers get any more of a head start."

I nod, already dialing Walsh's number.

"Where are you?" he demands, the minute he picks up. "I've been trying to reach you for the past half hour. The task force said you drove off with the suitcase."

I bring him up to speed on everything that's transpired, then forward him the video clip of Declan, and the pinned location where I made the drop. I wait on the line while he relays instructions to the task force over his radio.

"I've dispatched officers to the tower, although the kidnappers are likely long gone by now," he says. "I wish you'd let me know right away."

"I couldn't risk it. They've beaten Declan half to death already. He's running out of time."

"Have they messaged you, yet, with a location to pick him up at?" Walsh asks.

"No. The hour's just up. Should I text them?"

"Aye, you'd better."

I type out a message and watch the screen impatiently for a reply. "They're not responding."

"They might need some time to figure out a location to take him to," Walsh says. "Give them another thirty minutes and then try again. I'm heading back to the station right now. You should meet me there. That way you can ride with me to pick up your husband the minute you get the address."

I spend the next three hours sitting in an office at the station texting the kidnappers every twenty minutes or so, panic mounting inside me. "How long does it take to find a location to take Declan to?" I ask Walsh for the umpteenth time.

He shoots me a sympathetic look. "They might be waiting until nightfall to drop him off somewhere—easier to slip away under cover of darkness. I'm sure they'll be in touch soon. Once we get a description of the kidnappers from your husband, the task force will go after them. We'll have them in custody in no time."

He keeps trying to reassure me with platitudes, but I know from the hushed conversations he's having with the other gardaí that the situation is making them increasingly nervous. The intense media focus on the story of an American kidnapped while honeymooning in Ireland is only mushrooming as rumors of the ransom drop spread and morph into ever wilder stories. I've even been visited by a couple of local politicians offering their support and seeking a photo opportunity in the process.

At 5:00 p.m., I try texting the kidnappers again but this time I get an error message: *failed to send*. A sickening feeling spreads through me. "I think they shut the phone off," I tell Walsh, my words tumbling out. "I just tried texting them again and the message failed to send. Is your WiFi down?"

He checks his phone and shakes his head. "No, it's working fine." His eyes meet mine and I see a trace of pity in them.

"I have no way of contacting them now," I say. "How are we going to find Declan?"

"It's not uncommon for criminals to use multiple phones," Walsh replies. "They'll likely contact you on a different phone with an address to pick Declan up at. As soon as they do, we'll go after them and, hopefully, retrieve your money in the process."

"I don't care about the money. I just want Declan back safe."

My phone rings before Walsh can respond. My heart sinks when Brynn's name appears on the screen. I'd like nothing more than to ignore her call, but I promised her I would keep her updated on the drop, and she deserves the truth, hard as it might be to stomach. I take a deep breath before sliding my finger across the screen. "Hey, Brynn," I say, trying and failing to strike a neutral tone.

"Have they released Dad? Can I talk to him? Is he at the hospital?" Her words spill out, the questions hurled in panicked succession. When she finally pauses for breath, I give her the disheartening news. "I've made the drop. We're still waiting to hear back from the kidnappers, but they've disabled the phone they were texting me with."

"How are you going to find Dad if you've lost contact with them?" Brynn practically yells at me.

"Walsh thinks they'll use another burner phone once they're ready. They might be waiting until nightfall to drop your dad at an isolated location."

"You can't just do nothing until then!" Brynn cries. "Dad's injured. Don't you even care?"

"Your dad is all I care about right now," I say, with a weary sigh. "I've barely eaten or slept in days. I've handed out flyers, knocked on doors, given interviews, and paid the ransom. The gardaí are doing everything they can to locate him, too."

Walsh signals to me that he needs a word, and I end the call with Brynn, promising to contact her the minute I have any news.

"I'm sending a few members of the task force back to the farmhouse to sweep it," Walsh informs me. "There's a chance the kidnappers might have dropped Declan off there after we pulled out."

"I'll go with them," I say, jumping to my feet.

"It would be best if you wait here in case the kidnappers contact you with a different address," Walsh replies. "The farmhouse is a long shot. The likelihood of them returning to the same location is slim."

I sink back down in my chair, clutching my purse in my lap. The day is dragging on with no end in sight, and no hope on the horizon. So much has happened in the last twenty-four hours—none of it good. I've gone from assuming Declan got lost, to thinking he might have twisted his ankle and hoping the dog unit would find him, to dropping almost my entire nest egg in a ruined Celtic tower in a field, in the hope that the kidnappers who took my husband will spare his life.

So much for a fairytale honeymoon in Ireland. This country is threatening to make me a widow again.

10

_____

I'm back at the Airbnb when the long-awaited text finally comes through shortly after midnight from another unidentified number.

Your husband is in the parking lot at the cliff top trail at White Strand.

I jerk upright, my chest awash with erratic palpitations. I reread the text to make sure I'm not dreaming, and immediately dial Walsh's number.

"I'll send a garda car and ambulance right away," he says. "Meet you there in thirty minutes."

I stagger up from the couch where I've been slumped for the past couple of hours, utterly exhausted but unable to sleep. I'm apprehensive about navigating a stick shift on the narrow, unlit roads around here at night, but I'm unlikely to meet any other vehicles—no tractors, at any rate. Despite my misgivings, my insides are aglow with excitement at the thought of seeing Declan again. It was the right decision to make the ransom drop. Those thugs wouldn't have hesitated to kill him if I hadn't complied. I know it's unlikely I'll ever see my money again. If the police do manage to apprehend the kidnappers and recover any of it, it will be a bonus. Declan's life is more valuable than any amount of money, but I can't help feeling bad that everything Eric worked so hard for has either been taken by his unscrupulous partner, or stolen by the kidnappers.

I let loose a relieved breath when I make it safely to the junction and see the sign for White Strand Beach. Moments later, an ambulance with flashing lights races past me. My stomach muscles tighten. It's a stark reminder that Declan might be in bad shape. He could have serious internal injuries. Who knows how much they've been kicking him around or how severely they beat him? *Please don't die!* Tears scald my eyes and I blink to clear my vision. The last thing I need is to end up in the ditch again. At the rate I'm going, it's only a matter of time before I total the rental car.

It seems to take forever before I reach the cliff top parking lot. It's already a hive of activity. Three Garda cars, an ambulance and two unmarked vehicles light up the area. Shaking, I pull into an open spot and park haphazardly. I stumble out of the car and, without even pausing to close the door, run straight to the back of the ambulance. "Where is he?" I blurt out, my eyes darting between the two young paramedics standing to one side. "Where's my husband?"

"The gardaí are looking for him," one of them says, pointing to the trailhead.

I shake my head in confusion. "I don't understand. He was dropped off here in the parking lot."

The paramedics exchange blank looks. "You should probably talk to the gardaí," the other one says, at length.

I blow out a frustrated breath and hurry over to a garda I met at the station. He's talking on the radio, but he breaks off his conversation and turns to me, recognition flooding his face.

"What's happening?" I ask, unable to keep the panic out of my voice.

"We're conducting a search for your husband now. Walsh is on his way, and he's ordered search and rescue back out here."

"Search and rescue!" I exclaim. "Why—"

I wheel around at the squeal of tires. Walsh jumps out of a patrol car and strides over. He gives the other garda a curt nod, then turns to me. "Have the kidnappers contacted you again?"

"No." I drive my fingers through my tangled hair, shaking my head. "I don't understand. They said they dropped Declan off right here in the parking lot."

Garda Walsh rubs a hand over his stubble. "They may well have, but the fear is that Declan might have wandered off if he was in bad shape. I have search and rescue volunteers combing the beach as we speak, and gardaí walking the trail with searchlights."

A shiver runs through me as I picture a disoriented and injured—possibly concussed—Declan staggering along the cliff top trail in the pitch black of night trying to find his way back to the Airbnb. One horrific scenario after another floods my brain. My knees buckle beneath me, and Walsh reaches out to grab me as the blood drains from my head.

When I come to, I'm lying in the back of the ambulance being attended to by one of the paramedics. I moan softly as I attempt to sit up.

"Stay still," he chides me. "Your blood pressure's very low. You should try to eat something." He fishes around and produces a granola bar.

"My husband," I say weakly. "Have they found him?"

"They're still looking," the paramedic replies. "The canine unit arrived a few minutes ago." He hands me a paper cup of juice and helps support my head as I take a few sips. I lay my head back down and let out a ragged breath, closing my eyes briefly. I don't want to doze off in case I miss anything, but exhaustion is overpowering me like a hallucinogenic drug.

When I wake again, it's almost 5:00 a.m.

"Feeling any better?" the paramedic asks.

I sit bolt upright and grab him by the wrist. He shrinks back, gawping at me as though I'm a zombie coming back to life. I realize I must look like an unhinged mess. "Have they found him?"

His face clouds over. "They're still searching."

"I need to talk to Walsh." I slide off the bed and exit the back of the ambulance ignoring the paramedic's attempts to reason with me. The parking lot is packed with vehicles now. Tents have been set up, and the orange-vested search and rescue workers are bustling around like neon ants, communicating with one another on two-way radios. Even the media has descended, searching for a carcass to feed on.

My eyes flick desperately this way and that, looking for Garda Walsh. I finally catch sight of him in a patrol car talking on the radio. He glances in my direction, sensing my eyes on him. A stricken expression flickers across his face before he grooms his features to neutral. He climbs out and walks over to me. "That was the Coast Guard I was talking to. The helicopter will be here at first light. We'll be better able to spot your husband from the air."

Spot his body, you mean. I can feel the hope leaking from me. There's no reason to believe they'll find him. They didn't find him last time.

11

FOUR WEEKS LATER

I t feels altogether wrong to be sitting in the terminal at Shannon airport waiting to board a flight back to the States. Declan still hasn't been found, but I refuse to believe he's dead. I'm not convinced the kidnappers ever released him. Despite all their efforts to date, the gardaí have been unable to identify any suspects. They keep circling back to the ridiculous hypothesis that Declan set the whole thing up to get his hands on my settlement. It seems I'll be returning to the States robbed of my money and my husband, and without any hope of seeing either one again. I rummage around in my purse and pull out Declan's passport, tracing a fingernail over his face as I study his picture. I can't believe this man who promised to love and cherish me only a few weeks earlier betrayed me.

The elderly woman next to me leans over with an impish grin on her lined face. She gestures to Declan's passport. "My daughter married an American. This is my third trip over to see the grandkids in Santa Clarita. Were you here on holiday yourself?"

She smiles expectantly, reminding me of Moira

Murphy's good-naturedness, but everything about the friendliness of the Irish is intrusive now that I'm in so much pain.

"Business," I answer, abruptly getting to my feet and walking briskly in the direction of the restroom. Thankfully, the woman didn't recognize me from the news. I'm not ready to open up and tell my story to strangers. I have no words. I'm having a hard enough time psyching myself up to return to my life as I knew it. It's not the life I envisioned a few short weeks ago. I'm in a strange kind of limbo, a twilight zone of sorts—not officially, but possibly, a widow again—a widow with a stepchild who blames me for taking her dad away from her.

I keep my headphones on for the entire duration of the flight, limiting my interactions with others to innocuous courtesies when passing my food tray and trash to the flight attendant. When we land in Chicago where I'll catch my connecting flight to Los Angeles, I dutifully hand the immigration officer my passport. He studies my photo and then hands it back to me with a slight nod. "Welcome home, Ms. Evans."

I freeze when it hits me like a sledgehammer that I won't have to change the name on my passport now—or anywhere, for that matter. I may never become Mrs. Cafferty on paper.

The immigration officer raises a questioning brow and I throw a quick glance over my shoulder at the line of people waiting, before hurrying away from the booth. I feel lost and alone, bereft of the new identity I only recently embraced. Everyone around me appears to be striding purposefully through the terminal, but I feel as if I'm dragging my heels like a child who missed out on an adoption. The closer I get to home, the more I don't want to live the awful reality that awaits me. That's when it will really hit me. The stacks of sympathy cards, the pitying glances of my work colleagues, the eerily quiet house, sleeping alone each night, just like before.

But it's not only me I'm worried about. There's the question of how I'm supposed to comfort a grieving step-daughter who resents me. Brynn's broken, terrified her father is dead. Statistically speaking, she's probably right. But I can't admit that to her. My own heart wants to keep believing against impossible odds. I'm not giving up, not until I know for sure. I've already set up a website to keep people informed on developments in the story and I've done interviews with every Irish TV and radio station that would have me. Even now that I'm back in the States, I won't let the story die until Declan is found and I can bring him home.

After purchasing a latte at a coffee stand, I make my way to the gate for my connecting flight to Los Angeles. In the lounge area, I sink down in an open seat, too numb to do anything but scroll aimlessly through my phone. A gate agent announces a final boarding call for a flight to San Francisco at the gate next to mine. As I get up to toss my paper cup in the trash, a woman hurrying to board the flight, collides with me. "I'm so sorry," I blurt out, reaching out a hand to steady her. I gasp when I catch a glimpse of her face. My brain scrambles to make sense of what I'm seeing. I blink and do a double take. She looks just like her. But it's impossible.

"Excuse me," the woman mumbles, wrenching her wheeled bag around the luggage in her path. She takes a few more steps before I manage to find my voice. "Lynelle?"

The woman stops dead in her tracks, her head swiveling in my direction, a look of horror plastered on her face.

I don't know what prompts me in the moment, but I quickly raise my phone and snap a picture.

Too late, she attempts to shield her face as she gets in line to board the plane. My pulse races as I watch the gate agent scan her boarding pass. She doesn't turn around to look at me again before she disappears from view. She doesn't have to. I know who she was, and she knows I recognized her.

It was Lynelle Cafferty, *Declan's first wife.*

12

I stand stock still in the middle of the terminal, jaw
askew, trying to come to terms with the impossible.
Did I just watch a dead woman board a plane to San
Francisco?

"Excuse me, ma'am," an elderly man interrupts, tugging
gently on my sleeve. "Are you okay? You're white as a sheet.
You look like you've seen a ghost or something."

I blink at him, feeling as though an explosion has gone
off inside my head. "Maybe I have."

Without another word of explanation, I reach for my bag
and walk away, leaving the man speechless. I need to think.
Clearly, I'm not being logical. I'm an emotional basket case
—still in shock from Declan's disappearance. I've been
through so much lately and haven't been sleeping well. It's
entirely possible I'm imagining things, or I exaggerated the
resemblance to Lynelle in my mind. Maybe I superimposed
her face on a stranger's because I've been worrying about
how to navigate my reunion with Brynn. The fact that I can
never replace her mother is especially poignant in light of
Declan's abduction.

I pinch the bridge of my nose as I reason with myself. It couldn't have been her. Lynelle Cafferty is dead. She drowned three years ago. I breathe slowly in and out, trying to reconcile what I saw at the gate with what I know to be true. The odd part is that the woman turned her head when I called out to her. Why would she do that? Lynelle's an unusual name. Surely it can't be some kind of bizarre coincidence that a woman who's the spitting image of Declan's first wife also shares her name. Am I going crazy?

I wander around the gates in a daze, desperately trying to unknot my thoughts as I study the photo of the woman on my phone. I'm so wrapped up in trying to decipher what I saw, or possibly imagined, that I almost end up missing my connecting flight. By the time I land in Los Angeles, I can barely function between the jetlag, the heartbreak of losing Declan, dread at the impending reunion with Brynn, and the confusion turning my brain to mush. Kelly had offered to pick me up, but I turned her down, opting for an Uber instead. She's a beautician and she would have had to cancel an evening client to pick me up. Besides, I need to gather myself before I face anyone I know—even my best friend. I know I'll dissolve into a shivering wreck the moment she embraces me.

By the time I close the front door of my townhouse behind me, I'm weak with exhaustion. I leave my bag at the bottom of the stairs and go straight to bed. Tomorrow's a new day. I'll figure things out then.

WHEN I WAKE the following morning, the first thing I do is reach for my phone and make sure the photo I snapped at the airport is still there and that I didn't dream up the encounter in the terminal. The picture of the woman looms back at me, the shocked expression on her face captured perfectly. There's no question she looks a lot like the woman in Brynn's photo album. That thick, glossy dark hair and electric blue eyes is a stunning combination that's hard to miss. Maybe I can ask Brynn to show me her album again so I can discreetly compare it to the photo on my phone without telling her what I'm doing. She's dealing with enough trauma at the moment. I can't add to it with the shocking proposition that her mother has miraculously come back to life.

Realistically, I know that hasn't happened. The most likely explanation is always the simplest one. She's a woman who looks a lot like Lynelle. She probably turned her head because we'd just bumped into each other and she recognized my voice. In my heightened state of anxiety over Declan's disappearance, I actually believed it was his first wife. I close my camera App and toss my phone on the bed. It makes sense except for something Declan mentioned about Lynelle's drowning that's bothering me.

They never found her body, just one of her shoes.

A ripple of unease crosses my shoulders. What are the odds of both Brynn's parents going missing—possibly drowned? I toss the covers aside and make my way to the bathroom, acid churning in my stomach. Brynn's Aunt Jamie is dropping her back here tonight. The thought terrifies me. I don't know how I'm going to get through any of this, let alone help my distraught stepdaughter come to terms with it.

After showering and dressing, I decide to go into work for a few hours. I can't stand the deathly quiet that envelops the house, and I don't want to hang around all day until Brynn gets here. I might as well tackle the pile of work that's bound to have built up in my prolonged absence. Even if things are a hot mess, at least it will give me something to focus on, other than the burning pain that's eating through my heart like acid. With Declan gone, the grief of losing Aspen is more acute than ever. I miss the feel of her warm body tucked up next to me on the couch. I'm half-tempted to go by the shelter, but now's not the right time to bring a rescue dog into my life when I'm the one who needs rescuing.

I still haven't decided how much to share with my work colleagues. I'm sure they've been following the news and know all about the abduction and ransom. Walsh assured me he would keep me updated on the investigation, but I know how these things go. He's a busy man. He'll be patient for a few weeks, and then the updates will grow more and more infrequent, and my calls will become interruptions. Life goes on even though my world has come to a screeching halt.

When I walk into the office, Maddie rises from her desk, eyes widening. "Abby! I didn't expect to see you today! Didn't you just get back from Ireland?" She walks over to me and squeezes me tightly until I break away. Despite having worked together for years, the embrace feels awkward— how long do you hug someone who lost their spouse on their honeymoon?

"I can't sit around at home brooding over what happened," I say. "It's not healthy, and the house is unnaturally quiet. I'll grab a coffee and then you can brief me on where we're at with our ongoing projects."

Seated in my office a few minutes later, I sink back in my ergonomic chair, drawing comfort from the familiarity of my surroundings. My eyes land on a framed photo on the credenza. It's a picture of Declan and me at the beach, baseball hats on backwards, clutching oversized ice cream cones and grinning like school kids. That was the moment I realized I could actually be happy again, even if Eric wasn't a part of my future.

I startle when Maddie knocks on the door and comes in carrying an armful of file folders. "I don't know where you want to start," she says, placing the paperwork on my desk. "I brought everything so you can prioritize what needs to be done."

I reach for the file on top. "Let's go through them one-by-one and you can give me a rundown."

Maddie nods dubiously. "Are you sure you're up for this? I mean, you can take as much time off as you need."

"*This* is what I need," I say, flapping a file folder at her. "I have to focus on something other than whether Declan is dead or alive, or I'll go crazy."

"I can't tell you how sorry I am," Maddie says quietly. "We're all in shock. It's such an unbelievable thing to happen. I mean you hear of tourists being abducted in Mexico, but who would have thought it would happen in Ireland?" She gives a sad shake of her head. "I was so happy for you that you'd found love again after losing Eric."

I give a terse nod. It's too painful to think I might be widowed for the second time in a few short years.

"I don't mean to pry or anything," Maddie goes on, "but if you ever want to talk about it, I'm here for you."

I give a wan smile. "Thanks. I suppose you've been following the story on the Irish news sites."

"Everyone at the office has. I don't know how much of what they said was true—the whole hostage situation sounded crazy."

"It was true and crazy. To cut a long story short, the kidnappers demanded one-million euro for Declan's safe return. When I dropped the money off at the designated location, they texted me to let me know they'd left him in a parking lot at the top of the cliffs. We never found him. Everyone was out looking for him—the gardaí, search and rescue, a canine unit, volunteers—even the Coast Guard. I don't know if he's dead or alive. I haven't heard from the kidnappers since."

Maddie blinks, clearly shocked. "That's awful. I don't know what to say, Abby. You've been through so much already."

I exhale a heavy breath. "What makes it worse is that the Irish police are looking into the angle that Declan might have scammed me and taken my money."

Maddie's jaw drops. "That's outrageous! They wouldn't say something like that if they knew him."

"I agree. It makes no sense. Declan already had access to my money. He could have withdrawn it and disappeared without staging an elaborate kidnapping plot in a foreign country."

"Can you get the FBI involved?"

"I already contacted the state department while I was in Ireland. They put me in touch with a liaison officer. She's been talking with the embassy in Dublin, but it's not as if they're going to send a SWAT team over there to look for him."

Maddie's forehead creases. "Poor Brynn. It's unimaginable to think both her parents have disappeared without a trace. She must be devastated."

I'm tempted to tell Maddie about seeing Lynelle at the airport, but I bite my tongue. I need to do some investigating first. I can't let that kind of unfounded gossip spread throughout the office. If word gets out that Declan's first wife is alive and well, right after he disappeared with my money, it will be headline news on both sides of the Atlantic.

13

Shortly before five, I pull up outside El Castello restaurant where I've arranged to meet Kelly for an early dinner. I've been keeping her up to date on the investigation, but it's not the same as talking things over with her in person. I'm eager to see her and unload everything on someone I trust with my life, but I'm also dreading the possibility that I might fall apart entirely and become a blubbering mess. Granted, I've had a few weeks to come to terms with what has happened, but it was all so surreal in a foreign country, interacting with strangers, no matter how sympathetic to my situation. Moira Murphy even baked me a loaf of soda bread to take back to the States with me. I think I scared her when I hugged the still warm loaf to my chest and burst into tears. Declan never even got to taste her bread. Sometimes it's the little things that trigger my emotions.

Kelly is already seated in a booth at the far end of the restaurant. When she sees me, she jumps up and envelops me in her arms for the longest moment without saying a word. This time it feels right, and I hug her back, the tension in my shoulders easing for the first time in weeks.

"How are you coping?" she asks when she resumes her seat. "Dumb question, I know, but it sort of drips off the tongue at a time like this. I can tell you haven't been sleeping."

I reach for the glass of water on the table and take a sip. "I'm trying to hold it together, but honestly, I'm a mess. I just don't think I can go through this again. I can't bury another —" I drop my gaze without completing my thought. There's no need to with Kelly. We can finish each other's sentences.

She reaches across the table and squeezes my hand. "You're not there yet. One step at a time. Now that the embassy's involved, maybe they'll be able to find Declan and your money."

I shrug disinterestedly. "I don't care about the money. I just want my husband back."

A waitress breezes up to our table and we order a chicken pesto pizza to share and two Caesar salads.

"Do the Irish police have any leads at all?" Kelly asks.

"Nothing. Nobody saw or heard anything. It was early in the morning when Declan went out running, and the cottage was in a remote location." Even as the words leave my lips, I wonder again about the note that mentioned Shane. I've tried to write it off as a prank, but the niggling feeling that there's more to it has never left me.

Kelly shakes her head in wonderment. "Who would have thought something like this could happen in Ireland of all places? It's just so random."

"Speaking of random," I say, lowering my voice. "You're never going to believe who I saw in the terminal at Chicago airport."

Kelly arches a brow. "Someone famous?"

I grimace. "This beats famous. Think of someone who's dead."

Kelly blinks her fake lashes at me, barely able to restrain her curiosity as the waitress sets our plates down in front of us. The minute she moves away, Kelly leans across the table, a roguish look in her eyes. "Let me guess, Elvis?"

"It's not a joke. I'm hardly in the mood to goof off right now."

Kelly leans back in her seat, staring at me with a wounded expression. "You're the one who said you saw a dead person."

I pull up my phone and scroll through to the picture I took at the airport before passing it to Kelly. "Recognize this woman?"

She frowns in concentration. "She looks vaguely familiar, but I can't place her."

"It's Lynelle Cafferty—Declan's first wife!" I say. "Alive and well."

Kelly's eyebrows push against her Botoxed forehead. "Right!" She snorts and reaches for a slice of pizza, dropping it on my plate before helping herself to a piece.

"I'm serious!" I say.

"Abby, please. We both know that's not possible."

"I'm not wrong about this. I've seen plenty of pictures of Lynelle. Brynn even showed me an album she made of her mom. It's either her or her twin."

Kelly swallows a bite of pizza and then dabs at her lips, staining the paper napkin with her favorite Boss Babe mauve lipstick. "That's worth considering. We all have a doppelgänger. There's a limited number of genes in the gene pool, so it makes sense that if you shuffle the deck enough times, at some point, you're going to get someone who looks like you."

"A doppelgänger with the same name?" I say, picking at a piece of chicken on my plate. "I called out *Lynelle* when she was about to board the plane and she turned right around. You should have seen the look of shock on her face. She knew I'd recognized her."

Kelly opens her mouth to say something but appears to change her mind. She chews on her pizza for a minute or two in silence, before pushing her plate to one side. "Okay, suppose you're right. This is starting to get really weird. Declan disappears, along with your money, and then his first wife, who supposedly drowned, reappears. Are you connecting the dots here?"

I swallow a lump of congealed dough lodged in my throat. I know exactly what she's getting at. It's a theory I've been pushing back on ever since Walsh first floated it, but I can't deny I've had my doubts.

Kelly pulls her hair back, an earnest expression on her face. "What if this actually was a set up to scam you out of your money?"

I give a helpless shrug. "I have a hard time believing that. You should see the video the kidnappers sent. They beat Declan half to death."

"Let me see it," Kelly demands.

I pull it up on my phone and hand it to her.

Her lips tighten in a grim line. "It looks bad, but you'd be surprised what scammers do. They could have faked his injuries, or maybe he told them to beat him up to make it look more realistic."

"How can you even think that way about Declan? You know he's not that kind of man," I say. "Besides, he would never do that to Brynn. I don't believe that for a minute."

"And I have a hard time believing her mother faked her own drowning," Kelly says, reaching for her glass.

"You're right, it doesn't make sense," I say, tenting my fingers over my face as I try to clear my head. "I'm so confused. I don't know what to do."

"You need to hire a private investigator," Kelly says, her eyes lighting up. "The first order of business is to find out who this woman is. If Declan's first wife is still alive, that changes everything. You understand what I'm saying, don't you?"

Her eyes lock with mine, and I drop my gaze. I don't want to entertain the thought. It feels as though I'm betraying Declan for even thinking this way about him right when he needs me most. "I should go. I need to be back home before Brynn arrives."

"Want me to come with you?" Kelly asks.

I shake my head. "I need to do this alone. I'm sure Brynn has a thousand questions. I owe it to Declan to make sure she gets the answers she needs."

As I drive home, I mull over Kelly's suggestion to hire a PI. The thought already crossed my mind. I desperately want to know if it really was Lynelle Cafferty I saw at Chicago airport, but a part of me is afraid of what I might find out. I've been through loss before. I know how to move through it, pick up the pieces of life, and soldier on. But I don't know betrayal, and I don't think I could ever recover from finding out that Declan lied to me and our marriage was a sham.

Back in my townhouse I anxiously watch the clock in the kitchen, waiting on Brynn's imminent arrival. The burning question in my mind is where she's going to want to live now. Declan and I decided to sell his house and move into my townhouse as it's conveniently located for both our jobs. Brynn has already decorated her room and moved in most of her stuff, and the car Declan bought her for her sixteenth birthday is safely stowed in the parking garage. I don't know if she'll still want to stay here under the circumstances. But where else can she go? Her aunt has three small children of her own and she doesn't live in Brynn's school district.

Truth be told, I can't picture myself living in this house alone with Brynn for the next two years until she goes off to college. Although our relationship improved somewhat leading up to the wedding, it's tentative at best. I know she blames me for what happened to Declan. Honeymooning in Ireland was my idea.

The doorbell rings and I get to my feet feeling like a sack of wet cement as I trudge down the hallway. As I reach for the door, I remind myself that Brynn's a sixteen-year-old child wrestling with the very real possibility that she's now an orphan. What she needs most is to be loved. I wish I had some good news to share with her, but I haven't heard a whisper from Walsh since I arrived back in the States yesterday.

I'm tempted to tell her about bumping into the woman at the airport. But it would be too cruel in case it isn't what it seems. It's a secret I'll have to keep until I can get to the bottom of it.

14

I force my lips to smile as I pull open the door. Brynn stands on the front step trailing a backpack in one hand, a black beanie pulled down low on her forehead. Her Aunt Jamie hovers behind her, looking frazzled, one hand resting on a large, wheeled suitcase.

"Come in," I say, a telltale wobble in my welcome as we exchange awkward hugs of condolence. Brynn averts her eyes as she and Jamie follow me into the kitchen where we sit around the table, glancing uneasily at each other.

"I'm so sorry, Brynn," I say, leaning over to lay a hand on hers. She folds her arms in front of her, signaling in no uncertain terms that my touch is unwanted. Jamie throws me an apologetic look.

"Have you heard anything more?" Brynn asks.

"Not since I got back," I say. "But the Irish police promised to keep me updated."

"How are you holding up, Abby?" Jamie chimes in.

"Just trying to put one foot in front of the other. I really appreciate you stepping in and taking care of Brynn for me ... us," I correct myself.

Brynn glowers at me from beneath her beanie.

"I would have kept her longer, but she wanted to come here," Jamie says.

"I'm glad," I say, smiling at Brynn. "This is your home."

She gives a one-shouldered shrug.

"We can always work something out if she changes her mind," Jamie says.

"I won't. I told you I want to be here when Dad gets back," Brynn says.

"He'd like that. *I'd* like that," I hasten to add. "It's too quiet in the house by myself." That's not entirely true. Part of me dreads the thought of being left alone to make conversation with a sixteen-year-old who's determined to hold a grudge against me for marrying her father, not to mention losing him on our honeymoon. From her perspective, I suppose she has a point.

Jamie glances at her watch and gets to her feet. "I should get going. I promised the kids I'd be back in time to tuck them into bed. Please call me if there's anything I can do to help." She hugs Brynn goodbye, and I escort her to the door. "How's she coping with all of this?" I ask, lowering my voice.

"Not great, she's been acting up—lying to me about where she's going, locking herself in her room, talking on the phone with some friend I've never met." Jamie drags a hand across her brow. "I'm worried about her."

"I suppose it's only to be expected," I say. "This has got to be traumatic, especially after losing her mother."

"It's awful," Jamie agrees. "One minute she's certain her dad's dead and she's sobbing her heart out on the bedroom floor, and the next she's convinced herself he's going to be found. Her emotions are all over the place."

I exhale a tired breath. "I know how she feels. I'm either

clinging on to a thread of hope or drowning in a sea of hopelessness."

"It will be good for her to get back to school," Jamie says. "She misses her friends. She needs that social connection and their support."

I give a knowing nod. I can relate. Seeing Kelly tonight was hugely comforting even if she did raise more doubts about Declan.

"Please keep a close eye on her," Jamie says, slipping her purse over her shoulder. "You can't trust her."

I wave her off, then close the front door and take a deep breath before returning to the kitchen. "You know you can ask me anything," I say, sitting back down next to Brynn. "I want you to feel free to share all your concerns with me. We both love your dad very much, and I know we're experiencing a lot of the same feelings right now."

"You don't know *anything* about me," Brynn retorts, staring at her phone. "Why did you make him go there anyway? He wanted to go to Hawaii. It's your fault this happened."

I bite my tongue, reminding myself for the umpteenth time that she's a child lashing out from a place of pain. "I understand you're angry, but the police are doing everything they can to find your dad and—"

"Like what? They don't even know if he's alive."

I pick at my fingernail, trying to decide how best to answer that. Jamie and I agreed not to tell Brynn about the video of Declan—it would be too disturbing for her. "He's alive. The kidnappers let me speak to him," I lie.

Her fingers freeze mid-motion on her phone screen. "*What?*" She cuts me an icy glare. "Why didn't you tell me this before? What did Dad say?"

"That he was okay and that he loved us. They cut him off before he could say anything else." I frown at the phone in her hand. "That's new, isn't it? Where did you get it?"

Brynn gets to her feet abruptly. "I'm going to bed."

I grimace inwardly, berating myself for not keeping my mouth shut. Maybe her Aunt Jamie bought the phone for her. Either way, she's not in the mood to be interrogated. I wanted to take another look at the photo album of her mother, but given her frame of mind, that request's best left for another day. "See you in the morning," I call after her.

Ignoring me, she trudges up the stairs, her suitcase thudding defiantly on each step after her. I let my head sink into my hands. This is going to be every bit as difficult as I envisioned. For Declan's sake, I have to make it work. I brew myself a cup of Chamomile tea and sit down with my laptop. There's nothing more I can do to work on my relationship with Brynn tonight. In the meantime, I need to get to the bottom of who it was I saw at the airport. I open up Facebook and run a search for Lynelle Cafferty. Her old page pops up, but it hasn't been updated since her death.

I spend the next couple of hours browsing the internet, but I have no real idea how to go about looking for a missing person. I stumble across a couple of websites where you can pay for information, but the more I think about it, I should probably take Kelly's advice and hire a professional. If Lynelle Cafferty is alive, she's likely taken extensive steps to hide her true identity. An amateur like myself has little hope of finding her.

I turn my attention to procuring a PI and fill in a couple of online contact forms. Hopefully, one of them gets back to me, although this isn't the best way to go about finding someone reputable. I snap my laptop lid closed. I'm too exhausted to deal with this now. I'll put Maddie on it first thing tomorrow.

If Lynelle Cafferty is alive, we've all been living a lie. I only hope Declan wasn't a willing participant.

15

Brynn doesn't say much at breakfast, but she isn't quite as prickly as when she showed up on my doorstep last night.

"I know this is hard for you—it's hard for us both," I venture. "I was thinking it might be good to look through some photos together later. The wedding pictures came in. You looked beautiful that day."

"Okay, I guess," Brynn says, shouldering her backpack.

I try not to look too elated as she heads out to the garage. Looking through the wedding photos will give me the perfect opportunity to ask to see the album of her mother again.

After clearing away the breakfast dishes, I get ready and drive to the office, eager to get busy on my investigation into Lynelle Cafferty. "Maddie, can I have a word with you when you get a chance?" I ask, sticking my head into her cubicle in passing.

"Be right there," she replies, eying me curiously as she tries to read the expression on my face.

I leave my purse in my office and head to the break room to fetch a coffee. Catching the tail end of a conversation between two young data entry clerks, I hesitate outside the door.

"Can you believe that loser took her money and ditched her on her honeymoon? Bet he had a girlfriend on the side. What a jerk!"

Indignation wells up inside me. I suddenly feel as if all the emotions of the past few weeks are caught up in a vortex threatening to explode. Before I can think it through, I march into the break room, startling the two young women with my unexpected appearance. "How dare you trash my husband behind my back! For your information, Declan was kidnapped and beaten within an inch of his life." I pull up the video on my phone and stick it in front of their faces. "Does he look like someone who's cheating on his wife?"

They freeze, darting horrified glances between me and the screen, their faces blotchy with shame and shock. "I'm ... really sorry," one of them stutters. "We all are."

I ram my phone back into my pocket and stride across to the coffee maker. "Then how about you start praying for his safe return instead of bashing his reputation?"

The two clerks mumble another apology as they scuttle, red-faced, out of the office. I gulp down a shot of espresso and set my cup back beneath the spout to brew a second one, the tide of anger inside me deflating. I shouldn't have railed at them like that. It's human nature to be morbidly fascinated by sensational tales of thwarted love, and blood money. I groan inwardly as I rinse my cup in the sink—my outburst will just give the clerks more to gossip about.

When I get back to my office, Maddie is waiting for me.

"How did you sleep last night?" she asks.

"I blacked out," I admit. "I haven't slept that much in weeks."

"Good, you needed it. How did things go with Brynn?"

"She's taking it hard, naturally. She lashed out at me for talking Declan into going to Ireland on our honeymoon. Wrestling with her dad's abduction is bringing back painful memories of losing her mom." I rub a hand over my forehead, feeling the need to unload some of the weight I'm carrying. "I noticed last night she has a brand-new iPhone. She was very cagey about it when I asked her where she got it. I'm afraid she might have stolen it."

Maddie frowns. "Maybe you should take her to see a counselor. Does the school offer any services?"

I tap my fingers on the desk, considering the suggestion. "She might feel more comfortable talking to someone outside of school. Why don't you vet a few candidates for me?"

"No problem," Maddie replies, jotting it down on her notepad.

"While you're at it, I'd like you to find me a private investigator. Someone reputable and discreet."

She glances up, a puzzled look on her face. "Do you mean ... in Ireland?"

"No. Someone here who knows what they're doing, with experience in missing persons' cases." I clear my throat, feeling the need to explain myself. "They might be able to liaison with the Embassy and the Irish police for me."

"O-kay," Maddie says, sounding doubtful as she adds it to her notes. "That could get expensive if they have to fly over there."

"It's only to assist me stateside. Get me two or three good candidates. I'll take it from there."

After Maddie leaves, I reach for the pile of file folders on my desk. I'm absorbed in my work when my phone rings, a couple of hours later. I glance at the screen distractedly, intending to let it go to voicemail when I notice it's an overseas number. Tamping down the feeling of dread frothing up my throat, I take the call. "Hello?"

"Abby, it's Garda Walsh."

"Have you ... have they found him?" My voice comes out as a squeak, my chest constricting as I wait for his reply. *Please don't let him be dead.*

"No, I'm afraid not. But I had a visitor at the station who had some information relating to the case."

I rumple my forehead in confusion. "Someone from the embassy?"

"No. It was Moira Murphy. She found something after you left."

A wave of disappointment washes over me. I shut my eyes briefly, trying to remember what, if anything, I could have left behind at the Airbnb. "What was it?" I ask, feigning interest. All I want to hear is that they've found Declan, not my lost property.

"She was cleaning out the attic in her house and she came across a Rolex watch. To cut a long story short, Shane told her it was his."

My heart begins to pound more loudly as I try to track where the conversation is going. "I'm guessing he doesn't have the kind of money it takes to buy one."

"He has no money of his own," Walsh confirms. "Moira demanded to know where he got it from, and he told her a man approached him and offered him the watch in exchange for keeping an eye on you and Declan. He was supposed to text the man the minute either of you left the cottage alone."

I suck in a sharp breath, my thoughts hurtling back in time. "Was it the kidnappers' number?"

"Aye, same number. By the sound of it, they weren't targeting Declan in particular. Either one of you would have served their purpose."

I press a hand to my cheek, trying to come to terms with the idea that I could have been the one who was abducted. "Did Shane see what happened to Declan? Was he able to give you a description of the kidnappers?"

"He saw their vehicle. He was hiding behind a stone pillar at the bottom of the lane when they pulled up behind Declan in a dark gray Nissan van. He says two men jumped out and threw him in the back. There was a third man driving but they were all wearing ski masks. Shane was able to give us the license plate number but it turns out it was stolen so it doesn't help us."

"At least you finally have your evidence that Declan didn't stage the ransom," I say, in a barbed tone. "Clearly, he was taken against his will."

"I wouldn't jump to that conclusion, yet," Walsh says. "Recruiting Shane to witness the kidnapping could have been a clever ploy to lend authenticity to the scheme. The Rolex they gave him was a fake, not that he knew the difference."

I grip the phone tighter in my fist. Much as I hate to admit it, Walsh is right. This doesn't absolve Declan of suspicion in the eyes of the law. But it cements his innocence in my mind. My stomach churns as I picture him heading out for his run and suddenly finding himself being bundled into the back of a van. He would have been defenseless, dressed in running gear and a beanie, without as much as a phone for a weapon.

"Moira feels awful about the role Shane played in it,"

Walsh goes on. "She's helping him write a letter of apology. He also admitted to leaving that note on the sandwich table for you—it was his way of trying to tell you without actually telling you." Walsh gives a polite cough. "Moira would like to know if you intend to press any charges."

I allow a loaded pause, picturing Shane's eyes boring into me. It's his fault Declan was abducted. He betrayed us. He could have told me or Garda Walsh about the van a long time ago. We needn't have wasted all that time on a search and rescue mission at the cliffs when we should have been pursuing a stolen van. I don't care if Shane's simple-minded, or easily manipulated. And it doesn't matter how kind Moira has been to me. Declan's blood is on that stupid watch Shane traded for his life. I want him prosecuted.

I open my mouth to say as much when I suddenly remember Shane driving me home to the cottage in the rain, and the sadness in his eyes when he turned to me and stuttered: s-s-*some honeymoon, eh?* Did he really understand what he was doing when he agreed to exchange a text for a watch? Probably not. It would have sounded like an innocent enough request to an innocent soul like Shane. He wanted to tell me what he'd done afterward, but he was too scared. So he wrote the note instead. I can't bring myself to take my rage and frustration out on him. I'm ashamed enough of how I vented at the young clerks in the break room earlier. "There's nothing to be accomplished by pressing charges," I say at last.

"Very good. I know Moira will be relieved to hear that," Walsh says. "I'll ring again with any updates."

I hang up the phone and reluctantly turn my attention back to my work. Scanning through my inbox, I spot an email from Maddie titled: *recommendations*. I skim over the counselors' names and focus on the private investigators in the second half of her message. After spending a few minutes checking out each of the three websites, I pick up the phone and dial the only woman on the list.

There's nothing more I can do on my end to find Declan. I might as well put my efforts into tracking down his wife.

16

One week later, I find myself sitting across the desk from the private investigator I hired a few days earlier to find Lynelle Cafferty. Tonya Meyer is a no nonsense fifty-something-year-old ex-police officer who got straight to work with the little information I was able to send her, which amounted to nothing more than a handful of photographs, a copy of Lynelle's birth certificate that I discovered among Declan's files, and a flight number to San Francisco. Turns out Tonya was well worth the hefty retainer I paid her.

Her hazel eyes gleam with a hint of satisfaction behind heavy-rimmed glasses as she opens up a folder and throws me a conspiratorial look. "I have to admit I don't get these kinds of cases very often. Quite remarkable what a drowned woman can accomplish." She spins the file around to face me and taps a ragged fingernail on the top sheet. "April Monet she calls herself now. Got a nice ring to it. She's got taste, I'll give her that. She's employed as an administrative assistant at Gold Coast Auto in Missions Terrace—south-central San Francisco."

"And you're sure this is her?" I ask, glancing over the information.

Tonya picks up the folder and slides out a photo. "Take a look and tell me this isn't the same woman."

I pull up the photo on my phone and compare it to the one of April Monet exiting the car dealership. There's no mistaking it's one and the same woman.

"How did you manage to track her down?" I ask, replacing the photo in the folder.

Tonya's lips twitch into a catlike grin. "Connections. You can't get a hold of a flight manifest these days without them. After that, it was simply a process of elimination—weeding out passengers one-by-one. Once I'd identified her, I contacted an old colleague of mine who lives in the Bay Area. He drove to the dealership and took the photo for me."

"What about a home address? Did you find out where she lives?"

Tonya takes a cigarette from a pack next to her phone and lights up. I wrinkle my nose and discreetly scoot back in my chair. She gestures to the folder lying on the desk between us. "It's all there. Address—a rental—phone number, and email. She has no social media accounts under her new identity—clever girl."

I reach for the folder and slip it into my bag. "This is great. I'm amazed you were able to find her so quickly."

"If you want, I can arrange to have her surveilled," Tonya offers. "I'm not sure how you want to proceed, in light of your husband's disappearance." Her eyes narrow in shrewd appraisal. "Want me to try and find out if the two are connected in any way?"

"Sure, why not? I could use all the help I can get. The investigation into Declan's abduction is basically at a standstill. I set up a website to try and keep the story alive, but all

I get these days are weirdos posting comments, and occasional notes of condolence. The Irish police haven't been able to find any trace of him—they're leaning toward the theory that Declan scammed me and absconded with the ransom money. I'll give you my contacts over there. Maybe you'll have better luck than me getting answers."

Tonya takes a puff of her cigarette. "Leave it with me. What's your next move?"

"I'm going to show this photo to Lynelle's daughter, Brynn. If she confirms it's her mother, I'm going to the police."

Tonya scrutinizes me for a long moment. "You might want to hold off until you know more about the situation. People don't go to all those lengths to disappear without a good reason."

"This isn't only about Lynelle. I married a man I thought was a widower. If I've been deceived, I deserve to know the truth."

"Can't argue with that," Tonya replies, resting her cigarette in an overflowing ash tray. "All I'm saying is that you might want to hear her side of the story first before you involve the police."

On the drive home, I update Kelly on everything. I think she's more shocked than I am, but she has a client in her chair and can't speak freely. By the time I get back to the house, Brynn is home from school. The sting of acid creeps up my throat as I park next to her car in the garage. Just last night, we looked through her album again. I can't imagine what she's going to think when I show her this photo of her mother. I'm not sure she'll ever recover from her deception. I don't want to hurt her any more than she's already been hurt, but I can't hide the truth from her any longer. I'm convinced the woman is Lynelle Cafferty, and I need Brynn to confirm it.

"Hey! I'm home," I call out as I make my way to the kitchen where Brynn is seated at the table doing her homework.

"I thought you were going to work from home this afternoon," she says.

"I am," I say, setting my purse on the counter. "I had to run an errand on the way back. Are you hungry?"

"I was—I made a sandwich. I made one for you too." She gestures to a plate on the counter. "Turkey and Pepper Jack cheese."

I'm feeling too queasy to eat but I reach for the plate and sit down at the table next to her. "Thank you, that was thoughtful."

Brynn shrugs, then narrows her eyes at me. "What is it? You look like you want to say something."

I swallow the lump in my throat. "I need to show you something—a photograph—but I have to warn you, it might be upsetting." I hesitate. "Alarming even."

Brynn sets down her pen and gives me her full attention. "You're scaring me. Is this about Dad?"

"No! It has nothing to do with your dad," I reply, fidgeting in my seat. "Not exactly."

Brynn's brows shoot up. "I'm lost."

"I need to start at the beginning. When I was coming back from Ireland, my connecting flight went through Chicago. A woman accidentally bumped into me in the terminal and when I saw—"

Lynelle's face flashes to mind. I break off mid-sentence, suddenly unsure of what I'm about to do. This is going to rock Brynn's world. She's been on such an emotional roller coaster already that I'm not sure she can handle one more bombshell—it could be enough to send her over the edge. Thanks to Maddie, I've found a counselor for her, and she's agreed to go, but the first appointment isn't until next week. Until then, her wellbeing is wholly my responsibility.

"Well?" Brynn prompts, visibly irritated. "What were you going to say?"

I scroll through my phone to the picture I took at the airport and silently pass it to her.

She reaches for it, her face paling as her gaze zeros in on the woman on the screen. "Where ... did you get this?"

"I took it in the terminal at Chicago airport. I called out her name when she was boarding a flight to San Francisco and she turned and looked right at me." I allow a labored pause to pass before asking, "Brynn, is that your mom?"

"Yes." The word comes out as a decisive whisper.

I reach into my purse for the folder Tonya gave me and pull out the photo of April Monet. "Is this her, too?" I ask, holding it out in front of her.

The question hangs between us like a ticking bomb as I wait for her response. She stares at me, her eyes brimming with tears. "Is this ... real?"

Scooting over next to her, I wrap an arm around her shoulders. "It's real. She's been living in San Francisco under the name April Monet."

"How do you know all this?" Brynn asks.

I dig out one of Tonya Meyer's business cards and hand it to her. "I hired a private investigator to track her down."

Brynn flicks her thumb against the top of the business card, staring at it, trancelike. "The PI who found her—how did she do it?"

"I don't know all the in's and out's of how she gets her information, but she's an ex cop, so, presumably, she has contacts."

"Does she have an address for my mom?"

I nod. "She has all her contact details, although she's not on social media."

Brynn pockets the business card. "I want to go see her."

I exhale a long breath, relieved that she's reacting as calmly as she is. "I think we should go to the police first. We don't know exactly what's going on."

"Can we go tomorrow, first thing?"

"Absolutely. I'll call right now and make an appointment to speak to a detective."

"Can I keep the photo?" Brynn asks, clutching it to her chest.

"Sure. Just don't lose it. We'll need to bring it with us tomorrow, along with that photo album you made of your mother. The police will want to compare the pictures."

"Okay." Brynn checks the time on her phone and begins stuffing her books into her backpack. "I have to go. I'm spending the night at a friend's house. We're working on a joint project for biology class."

"Whoa! Wait just a minute!" I say, holding up a hand. "We need to talk about this, first. What's this friend's name?"

"Carrie," Brynn calls over her shoulder, grabbing a water bottle from the fridge.

"Carrie who?"

"Carrie Bleeker. She's in my class. I've stayed there a million times before. Dad knows her parents."

"Where does she live?"

Brynn rolls her eyes. "903 Alpine Drive. It's literally five minutes from here. Dad lets me sleep over all the time."

I press my lips tightly together as I verify the location on my phone. "All right. Just make sure you answer your phone if I call. And don't show that photo to Carrie, or mention anything about it, until we've talked to the police."

"I'm not going to say anything. I'm not that stupid."

I give her a tight smile. "We'll get to the bottom of it, I promise—starting tomorrow."

"I gotta go," she says, throwing her backpack over her shoulder. "I'll be back in the morning to shower before we go to the station."

She bounces out the door and slams it behind her. A shiver crosses my shoulders as her Aunt Jamie's words float to mind. *She's been lying to me about where she's going ... talking on the phone with some friend I've never met.*

I study the address on my phone, wondering if I should drive by later and make sure Brynn's car is there. I make a mental note to find out who Carrie Bleeker is. At all costs, I have to keep Declan's daughter safe.

The last thing I need is for her to disappear too.

17

True to her word, Brynn is home the following morning by 7:00 a.m. sharp.

"Get your project finished?" I ask, in between bites of toast.

"Yep. It took us 'til midnight," she says, before running upstairs to shower.

I've already left a message with her school to let them know she'll be coming in late this morning. Thankfully, they've been very accommodating with her haphazard schedule over the past few weeks. They've even agreed to let her out early on Mondays so she can make it to her counseling appointments.

"You have the photo with you, right?" I ask, as I back the car out of the garage.

Brynn pats her backpack in her lap. "Right here."

Neither of us say much on the drive to the police station. I'm too busy mulling over how best to explain my suspicions to the police. It all seems so outlandish. My mind turns over everything Declan told me about his first wife. He hinted, more than once, that she might have committed suicide.

Was he deliberately trying to mislead me, or was he fooled by Lynelle, too?

When we pull up outside the station, I switch off the engine and turn to Brynn. "Honey, I know you're hopeful, but you need to be prepared for anything. If it turns out this is your mother, there must be a pretty compelling reason she hasn't tried to contact you in the past few years. Maybe she's not in a good place. You should brace yourself in case this isn't the happy reunion you're envisioning."

"I don't care. I just want to see her."

I squeeze her hand before she has a chance to snatch it away. "If it's your mom, I'll take you to her, I promise you that."

Inside the police station, we're left waiting on thin, vinyl chairs in the reception area for what seems like forever before a desk officer escorts us down the hall to meet the detective I spoke to on the phone. He stands and reaches out a burly hand to greet us as we enter his office. "Sorry to keep you waiting. I'm Detective Rod Hurley, pleased to meet you both." He towers over us, oozing confidence as he gestures for us to take a seat. "By the sound of it, this is a pretty intriguing case all round. Why don't you start at the beginning and tell me exactly what's going on?"

Brynn throws me an unspoken plea to do the talking.

I spend the next few minutes filling the detective in on everything I know about the circumstances surrounding Lynelle's death, allowing Brynn to chip in here and there along the way. "When I was flying back from Ireland, my connecting flight went through Chicago," I say, pulling out the photo of Lynelle on my phone. "I recognized Declan's first wife from her Facebook profile and the photo album Brynn showed me. I couldn't believe what I was seeing. I was pretty traumatized, coming back from Ireland after my husband—" My voice breaks and I twist my hands in my lap, sensing an all too familiar prickling in my eyes.

"Right. We'll get to that in a minute," Detective Hurley interjects smoothly. "You mentioned you hired a private investigator and she managed to dig up some information."

Brynn pulls out the photo Tonya gave me and slides it across the desk. "This is my mom," she says, holding the detective's gaze. "I'm sure of it." She reaches into her backpack for the photo album and sets it on the desk. "You can compare it to these pictures of her."

Hurley takes the photo and holds it next to the one on my phone screen, then flicks through a few album pages. "It certainly appears to be the same woman," he concurs. "Let me have one of my tech guys take a quick look."

He exits the room with the photos and returns a couple of minutes later. "They're doing a preliminary analysis right now. We have some pretty slick facial recognition software." He tents his fingers on the table in front of him. "Now, tell me about your husband."

I take a shallow breath before I begin. "Declan and I were married five weeks ago. We went to Ireland on our honeymoon. We had rented a little stone cottage in the countryside near the west coast." I pause for a moment, scrunching my eyes shut as the memory of waking up alone in bed on the other side of the Atlantic Ocean hits me again. "When I woke up the first morning, Declan wasn't there. I wasn't overly concerned, initially. I assumed he was training because his running shoes were gone."

"Is that usual for him?" Hurley asks.

"Yes. He's training for a marathon and we'd agreed he would stick to his schedule while we were in Ireland."

I proceed to describe the aftermath of Declan's disappearance—the extensive search and rescue mission, the strange note Shane admitted to writing, the kidnapping he claimed to have witnessed, and the ransom money I paid to the kidnappers.

Detective Hurley lets out a low whistle. "That's a lot of money. Do the Irish police have any leads?"

"None. The embassy in Dublin has been in touch with the FBI but, unless you're someone famous or a minor child, they have limited resources to throw at what essentially amounts to a dead end as far as they're concerned."

Hurley grunts. "Who's your local contact in Ireland?"

"Garda Walsh. He's doing his best but he's a rural police officer. He's in over his head."

"I'll need his phone number. Also the contact info for the couple who run the Airbnb you stayed at. I'd like to talk to them, too."

I pull out my phone and rattle off the information. "Good luck with the accents."

Hurley drums his fingers on the desk. "Do you think there's a connection between Lynelle showing back up and Declan's disappearance?"

I throw a covert glance at Brynn. I don't want to talk about my suspicions in her presence. She doesn't need to be party to me throwing her parents under the bus.

Sensing my hesitation, Hurley turns to her, "Can I ask you to wait in the reception area for a few minutes while I talk to your stepmom?"

Brynn curbs a scowl as she gets to her feet. "Will you let me know when the tech guy comes back?"

"Absolutely," Hurley assures her. He ushers her out of the room and closes the door behind her. "I know this is painful," he says, slumping back down in his chair. "But I'm sure this isn't the first time you've been asked this. Is there any possibility at all that Declan and his first wife were involved in some sort of scheme to get their hands on your money?"

"I know what it looks like, but you don't know my husband. He would never betray me like that—or his daughter. Did you watch the video I sent you last night? The kidnappers beat him half to death."

Hurley fingers his jaw. "I watched it, but these things can be staged. I've seen this kind of scam play out before. Lonely widow with means is swindled out of her savings by a fraudster playing the part of loving husband 2.0 material."

"Lynelle disappeared years ago," I point out. "It doesn't make sense. They can't be working together."

Hurley folds his arms across his chest and leans back in his chair. "It might not be the first time they've tried it."

I shake my head. "I don't believe it. I hate that Declan's reputation is being dragged through the mud like this. I just want you to get to the bottom of why Lynelle Cafferty faked her death and is living under a false identity. Brynn and I deserve to know the truth."

I look up at a sharp knock on the door. A young officer beckons to Hurley. "Give me a minute," he says, getting to his feet.

I sink back in my chair fighting my frustration. Why does everyone assume Declan's disappearance has something to do with Lynelle? Even Kelly has lost faith in his innocence. I squeeze my hands in my lap, tears stinging my eyes. Maybe I am ignoring the obvious. Maybe it's time to give up on Declan.

I'm lost in my thoughts when Hurley strides back into the office with a baggie containing my phone, and the photos. "That was my tech guy," he says. "I have good news and bad news."

"Let's start with the good," I say. "I've had enough bad news to last me a lifetime."

He fixes a sympathetic smile on his lips as he settles back into his chair. "The good news is that it's definitely the same woman in all the photos. The bad news is that the photo the PI gave you is a fake."

18

Detective Hurley opens the baggie and pulls out the photo Tonya gave me. He lays it flat on the desk between us. "Take a look at the unnaturally smooth edges around her hair and face. She's been superimposed on the scene. It's easy enough to swap someone's face out in Photoshop."

I shake my head in disbelief. "That doesn't make sense. Why would a PI give me a Photoshopped picture?"

Hurley hefts a shaggy brow. "I take it this was a reputable PI you hired and not some kook trying to make a few extra bucks on the side?"

"My personal assistant vetted her for me. I checked out her website myself and she had glowing reviews. She wasn't cheap but she was efficient. I was impressed at how quickly she managed to track Lynelle down and get the information for me."

Hurley grunts. "Might be a red flag right there."

I frown, trying to make sense of it. Why would Tonya risk her reputation by doing something so stupid? "She said an old colleague of hers in San Francisco drove to the dealership and took the photo. I suppose he could have doctored it without her knowledge to make a few bucks."

Hurley doesn't look convinced. "Any PI worth their salt would have noticed the discrepancy as soon as they looked at the photo."

"Will you follow up with the contact information at least?" I ask. "The PI gave me Lynelle's address in San Francisco."

Hurley scratches his stubble. "I can't waste resources if the photo's fraudulent. You're going to have to give me more than this to go on before we dispatch officers to look for her. I suggest taking the photo back to your PI and getting some answers, first." He glances at his watch and throws me an apologetic look. "I need to get going. Call me once you hear back from the PI."

I get to my feet, swaying unsteadily. This is a twist I hadn't anticipated. And now I'm going to have to break the news to Brynn that the PI directed us down a dead end. I groan inwardly. I wish I'd held off on involving her until I was sure of my facts, but how could I have anticipated this outcome?

Brynn jumps to her feet the minute she sees me. "What did the tech guy say?"

I grit my teeth, unable to meet her eyes. "I'll tell you about it in the car."

"Wait! Aren't they going to help us?"

"It's complicated," I say, exiting the police station.

I press my key fob to unlock the car and slide in behind the wheel.

"What did they say?" Brynn demands, the minute she climbs in.

I grip the steering wheel, steeling myself for her reaction. "The photo the PI gave me was edited. Someone superimposed your mother's head onto a woman exiting Gold Coast Auto."

"What?" Brynn cries out. "Why would the PI do that?"

I rub my temples to relieve the tension. "That's what we need to find out."

"Then call her! Now!" Brynn shouts. "Or I will." She unzips the front pocket on her backpack and pulls out Tonya Meyer's business card. I watch with apprehension as she taps in the number on her phone and hits the speaker. It rings and rings and finally goes to voicemail. Brynn thrusts the phone into my hands. "Leave her a message. She doesn't know who I am."

"Hey Tonya," I say, holding the phone close to my lips. "It's Abby Cafferty. Can you give me a call as soon as you get this. It's about the photo of April Monet. I talked to the police this morning and they're telling me it's been edited. Please call me back as soon as possible so we can sort this out." I press end and eye the phone curiously before handing it back to Brynn. "You never did tell me where you got this."

Brynn glares at me. "*That's* what you're worried about. I wish you cared half as much about Mom as you do about a stupid phone."

"I *do* care, but there's nothing more we can do in the meantime," I say, starting up the car.

After I drop Brynn off at school, I head into work. My thoughts are spinning like balls in a bingo cage. I have no idea how to get to the bottom of what's going on, and apparently, neither do any of the professionals I've engaged. Could Declan's disappearance and Lynelle's reappearance really be connected? Detective Hurley seems to think so.

Garda Walsh suspected as much. Even Kelly is looking at Declan through a whole new lens. Have I been played for a fool?

Sequestered in my office, I throw my purse on a chair in the corner. I have more than enough work piled up on my desk to distract me for the next few hours. I fire up my computer and dive in before I get lost in my despairing thoughts again. Shortly after 3:00 p.m. I get a call from Brynn's school. Goosebumps prick my arms. What now? Maybe I shouldn't have forced her to go to school after what happened this morning. With an air of dread, I pick up the phone.

"Hi Abby, it's Terry Kerr, Brynn's home room teacher. I know you said she would be a little late today so when she didn't show up, I thought I'd give you a quick call and make sure everything was okay. I was worried she might have got bad news about her dad this morning."

"What do you mean she didn't show up? I dropped her off a little after 10:00 a.m."

There's a beat of silence on the other end of the line. I scrunch my eyes shut, fear blistering its way across my shoulders. *Please don't tell me Brynn has disappeared too.*

"I ... checked with all her teachers," Terry says, sounding unsure of herself. "She didn't show up for any of her classes."

I grip the phone tighter in my fist. "Maybe she walked home after I dropped her off. She's upset about the lack of progress with the investigation. I'll try calling her right now. Thanks for letting me know." I'm about to end the call when something occurs to me. "By the way, do you know who she's been hanging out with at school? She mentioned a Carrie Bleeker—she's been round at her house working on a project, but I've never met her. I'm worried because she's been so withdrawn lately."

"Carrie Bleeker? Just a minute."

I hear a faint tapping in the background and then Terry comes back on the line. "I knew I didn't recognize the name, but I wanted to check our records to be sure. I'm afraid we don't have a Carrie Bleeker enrolled here."

19

The minute I hang up with the school, I dial Brynn's number. Despite repeated attempts to reach her, she doesn't pick up, so I send her a flurry of panicked texts. Relief floods through me when, at last, I see three little gray bubbles dancing below my latest message. She's reading it, so at least that means she's okay. Moments later, her response pops up on my screen.

At Carrie's. Be home for dinner.

I stare at my phone with a growing sense of unease. Why is she sneaking around behind my back? And who is this Carrie Bleeker? On impulse, I do a quick search on Facebook. Only one Carrie Bleeker shows up in the results and she's closer to my age than Brynn's. I scroll through the other names that pop up. *Carey Bleeker, Carolyn Bleeker, Carrie Beeker, Corrie Bleeker.* None of them are teenagers. Either she's not on Facebook or Brynn gave me a false name. I scrub my palms over my face, dreading the thought of confronting her. Should I text her back and let her know her behavior is unacceptable? I could drive over there right now and pick her up, but it will only enrage her—she might refuse to come home at all.

I drum my fingers on my desk, agonizing over my next move. It's probably best to wait until dinner and confront her in the safety of my own home. I'm beginning to suspect she's been hanging out with a boy this whole time. Declan would be furious if he knew I'd allowed her to sleep over at some strange guy's house. I need him here to handle this. I have no experience with teenagers. Exiting out of Facebook, I open up my calendar and double check the counseling appointment I set up for Brynn. Monday can't come fast enough as far as I'm concerned.

I make a half-hearted attempt to return to my work, but I can't seem to concentrate on anything other than checking my phone incessantly. Tonya still hasn't returned my call. Apparently, getting scammed out of my money is becoming a pattern. After pacing across my office for several minutes, I snatch up my purse and keys. I'll drive by Tonya's office and see if I can catch her. She could be deliberately ignoring my call, or she might be trying to get to the bottom of why her contact in San Francisco doctored the photo. Either way, I can't sit around wondering any longer. I need answers.

Half an hour later, I pull into the parking lot of the building where Tonya Meyer's office is located. I lock the car and make my way up the outdoor staircase to the second floor. Her office is at the far end of the breezeway, but I can already see from here that there are no lights on. I walk down to her door and reach for the handle. That's when I see the note taped to the door.

Office closed until further notice due to family emergency.

No! I let out an exasperated grunt. You have *got* to be kidding me! What are the odds? I can't seem to win for losing. I kick the door in frustration before returning to my car. On the drive home, I mull over my next step. The odds are stacked against me. My PI has gone AWOL. Detective Hurley has reversed course on assisting with the investigation, thanks to the fake photo. Walsh is clearly in over his head, and the state department, the Embassy, and the FBI aren't interested in another People magazine filler story. That leaves me. I swore I wouldn't let this story die. And it's not just any story—Declan's my husband. If I want answers, it looks like I'm going to have to get them myself. I'll start with the information in the folder from Tonya Meyer. Maybe the photo was edited, but that doesn't necessarily mean it was for nefarious reasons. Perhaps Tonya's contact didn't get a clear shot of Lynelle exiting Gold Coast Auto and decided to merge two photos he'd taken. There could be a perfectly simple explanation. More important, the contact information might still be good.

The minute I get home, I pull out my phone and call Kelly. "I need a huge favor."

"For you, anything," she replies. "You could use a session in my chair—how about some highlights?"

"I was thinking more along the lines of a babysitting gig. I need you to look after Brynn for a couple of days."

"You're joking, right? You're asking a woman who has never even been married to babysit a mutinous teenager who's lost both her parents?"

"It's only until tomorrow night," I plead. "I need to fly up to San Francisco this evening and check out the address the PI gave me."

"Can't she get her associate up there to do that?"

"She's not answering her phone. I went by her office and there's a note on the door saying the office is closed due to a family emergency."

"What? The PI's MIA now too?" Kelly gasps. "This is

turning into a crime show special."

"Tell me about it. I've just become the chief investigator."

"Are you sure about flying up to San Francisco?" Kelly asks. "What if it really is Lynelle, and she and Declan are running some kind of scam? She could be dangerous—*they* could be dangerous."

"I'll pack my pepper spray if it makes you feel any better."

"You can't take that stuff on the plane," Kelly grumbles.

"Fine! I'll buy some when I get there. Are you going to help me or not?"

"You'll definitely be back tomorrow night?" Kelly asks, already sounding remorseful for giving in.

"Yes. I promise. I'll send you my flight details. You and Brynn can pick me up when I get back. One more thing. I can't tell her where I'm going or she'll want to come. We need to tell her it's a business trip."

Kelly lets out a resigned sigh. "Packing my overnight bag as we speak."

I hang up and pull out my laptop to book a flight and hotel. I can catch a 9:30 p.m. flight that will get me in to San Francisco at 11:00 p.m. That will give me enough time to eat dinner with Brynn this evening and let her warm up to the idea of Kelly spending the night. It helps that she's a beautician and Brynn's a makeup junkie. I won't broach the subject of Carrie Bleeker's true identity tonight. The last thing I need is for Brynn to storm out and disappear. I'll save that conversation until I get back. One crisis at a time.

I'm stirring a pot of chili at the stove when Kelly shows up a little after 5:00 p.m.

"I really appreciate you doing this," I say, as we embrace.

"Let's just hope I don't live to regret it." She dips a spoon into the chili and blows on it before tasting it. "Yum. This is why I'm not married. Nobody's impressed when I tell them I have ninja microwaving skills."

"Okay, listen up," I say, putting the lid back on the chili. "Let's go over a few ground rules before Brynn gets here."

"Shoot," Kelly says, helping herself to a glass of water.

"Homework before TV. No going over to friends' houses, not even for an hour, or to pick up a textbook, or for any other lame reason, and definitely no sleepovers. She goes to school in the morning whether she wants to or not. And you need to call the school to confirm she showed up for classes —she skipped today."

Kelly arches a perfectly penciled brow. "You weren't joking when you said it would be a babysitting gig."

I grimace. "I'm just trying to protect her—I'm not sure what from, yet, but she's hiding something from me. I think she might have a boyfriend, someone her father and I wouldn't approve of."

"*Now* you're talking my language." Kelly gives me an elaborate wink. "Don't worry, I'll wheedle it out of her. I brought my bag of tricks. I'll give her a smoky eye and sweet-talk her into spilling her secrets. Clients can't resist my charm once I have them in my chair."

I blanch at the sound of a key turning in the front door. "Brace yourself. She's home."

"Hey, Kelly," Brynn says, when she walks into the kitchen. She tosses her backpack in the corner and opens the refrigerator, rooting around for something to drink. "Are you staying for dinner?" She opens a Gatorade and sinks down at the kitchen table.

Kelly grins. "As a matter of fact, I am."

I turn back to the stove and begin ladling the chili into bowls. I'll break the news to Brynn that I'm leaving once we're seated around the table. If I tell her now, she might throw a tantrum and make a beeline for her room. "Brynn, would you grab the sour cream and cheese from the fridge, please."

"I love how you've done your hair," Kelly says, when Brynn resumes her seat at the table. "I brought my makeup bag. We can play around with a whole new look this evening, if you don't have too much homework that is."

Brynn shrugs, looking chuffed. "Sure, if you have time."

I pass out the bowls and take a seat. "Actually, Kelly's going to be spending the night. I have to catch a flight to San Francisco. I have a business meeting in the morning."

Brynn puckers her lips. "I don't need someone to babysit me."

I fix her with a stern look. "Apparently, you do. You bailed on your classes today and went to a friend's house without permission."

Brynn scowls. "I was bummed about the fake photo, that's all. Doesn't mean I need a chaperone to put me to bed and get me up in the morning."

"It was my idea to hang out," Kelly soothes. "I thought it might be fun for us to have a spa night while Abby's out of town." She winks at Brynn, and to my relief, her shoulders relax.

The rest of the dinner goes off without a hitch. After I've cleared the dishes and loaded the dishwasher, I order an Uber. Brynn and Kelly pull out an array of cosmetics at the kitchen table, chattering away like bosom buddies. I smile to myself as I reach for my overnight bag. With a bit of luck, Kelly will prove to be every bit the resourceful mole she bragged she could be.

If she can get to the bottom of the Carrie Bleeker mystery while I hunt down Declan's first wife, it will be a two for one.

20

<hr/>

By the time I get through all the paperwork associated with the rental car and find my way from the San Francisco airport to the hotel, it's almost midnight. I place the file with all the information the PI gave me on the nightstand. It's pretty clear from Tonya's research that April Monet didn't exist until a few months after Declan's first wife supposedly drowned. April aka Lynelle is going to have a hard time talking her way out of this. My plan is to get up early and try and catch her at her house before she leaves for work. She's unlikely to open up to me surrounded by colleagues and customers at the auto dealership. To have any chance at all of getting the truth out of her, I need to catch her alone. I want to know why she faked her death, more important, I need to know if Declan was in on it. After that, I'll decide what to do about it. There's always a chance she'll try to deny she's Lynelle Cafferty, but she can't deny it's her face in the photos.

My alarm goes off the following morning at 5:30 a.m. I groan and force myself out of bed. According to Tonya's information, Lynelle starts work at 8:30 a.m. I checked the route last night, and the drive from her home to Gold Coast Auto takes an average of thirty minutes. I plan to be at her house long before she leaves for work to give us ample time to talk.

After a quick shower, I grab a muffin and coffee from the breakfast cafe in the hotel lobby and punch in Lynelle's home address on Apple Maps. My heart hammers beneath my thin sweater as I drive. What happens next could upend my life in the worst possible way. I've already resigned myself to the idea that she's alive, but if it turns out Declan has been in cahoots with her, I don't think I'll ever be able to get over the betrayal. A little before 6:45 a.m. I turn onto Lynelle's street and park a few houses down from her place. Pretending to be engrossed in my phone, I stroll up and down the street, surreptitiously stealing glances at 3490 Fairmount. There's a light on upstairs and it isn't long before I spot the lights turning on downstairs too.

A dinged-up blue Chevy Malibu is parked in the driveway. I don't know for sure if Lynelle is the only person who lives here, which is something I didn't consider before. Too late now to second guess myself. I watch as a balding man juggling a briefcase and a travel coffee mug comes out of the house next door and gives me a distracted nod before climbing into his car and driving off. I can't hang around on the street too long or I'll start to attract the attention of the neighbors—it's now or never.

Summoning my courage, I walk up to the front door and ring the bell, shifting from one foot to the other as I wait. After several minutes go by with no response, I try the bell again. This time I detect footsteps approaching the door. A moment later, it swings open to reveal a familiar-looking woman dressed in black slacks and a teal sweater set. She tugs distractedly at her dark hair which she appears to be in the process of curling. Her startling blue eyes light on me, then widen in alarm. I stare back at her, momentarily stunned that the contact information Tonya unearthed was valid. It's definitely Lynelle. She makes a move to slam the door, but I plant my foot on the threshold. "I know you recognize me. You bumped into me in the terminal in Chicago. Please, Lynelle. I know it's you. You were married to Declan Cafferty. We need to talk."

"I don't know anyone called Lynelle," she replies, her eyes cold as ice cubes.

"Declan's missing. He was abducted in Ireland."

She shakes her head in disgust, looking me up and down in an exaggerated fashion. "Is this one of those ridiculous scams to send money to relatives in trouble overseas? Who are you?"

"I'm his wife. His second wife. At least I thought I was. But it turns out you're not dead, after all, so I'm not sure where that leaves me."

Fear flickers in her expression, but when she speaks, her voice cuts like steel. "You're crazy. Get off my doorstep or I'm calling the police."

I raise my brows. "I doubt you'll do that, considering you're the one who's committed a crime."

I glance across the street as three young kids come running out of the house opposite Lynelle's.

"Hurry up and get in the car," their mother yells from the doorway. She waves across at us before abruptly turning and disappearing back inside the house.

"You have sixty seconds to get off my property or I'll tell my neighbor you're harassing me," Lynelle hisses at me. "I'll scream for help if I have to."

Reluctantly, I remove my foot from the doorframe. "All I'm asking for is the truth. I don't care what you've done. I only care about Declan." I hesitate before adding, "Don't you have any feelings at all for your daughter? Do you have any idea how much Brynn has suffered over the past few years thinking you're dead all this time?"

Lynelle's face tightens. "I don't know who you're talking about."

Her neighbor reappears in her doorway holding a mop and hurries across the street to us. "I meant to return this last night. Thanks for the loan, April," she says, giving me a curious once over.

I nod in greeting as I walk briskly away. The last thing I need is a nosy neighbor inserting herself into the situation. I'll wait until she drives off and then try talking with Lynelle again. I stroll to the end of the street while they continue to chat. When I turn back around, I spot Lynelle climbing into the Chevy Malibu in her driveway. I grit my teeth in frustration. No doubt, she's heading in to work early in an effort to avoid me. But she can't run from me forever. I know where she works and if that's how she wants to play it, so be it.

I drive into town and order a bacon-and-egg breakfast in a small nondescript cafe where I mull over my options. It's gearing up to be a long day and I need to come up with a new plan now that I've lost the element of surprise. I can't confront Lynelle at Gold Coast Auto. She could have me escorted off the premises for trespassing. I need to try and catch her on her lunch hour. I pull out the file folder and review Tonya's comprehensive report. It appears Lynelle takes her lunch at the same time every day—a creature of habit. A rookie mistake. If you don't want to be found, you need to vary your routine. Even I know that much.

I check the time and then give Kelly a quick call. "How's everything going with Brynn?"

"Smooth as butter. We gave each other facials, I taught

her a few new makeup tricks, she did her homework, went to bed at a reasonable hour, got up on time, and even checked into her classes. I grade myself an A."

I chuckle. "Don't be so hard on yourself. I'd give you an A+. Did you manage to find out anything about who she's been hanging out with—the mysterious Carrie Bleeker?"

"No, but I'm pretty sure Carrie's not a boyfriend."

"How do you know?"

"Because she told me about a boy in her class she likes. She's hoping he'll ask her to the school dance."

"That's a relief, but I'm still concerned about Carrie being a bad influence. Keep prodding. Maybe she'll open up to you some more."

"Any luck on your end?" Kelly asks.

"Only the bad kind, so far. I went to Lynelle's house this morning and knocked on her door. She completely blew me off, denied she was Lynelle Cafferty—even pretended she didn't know who Brynn was."

"Did you show her the photos?"

"I didn't get a chance. Her neighbor interrupted us. I'm going to try and catch her when she takes her lunch instead."

Kelly gives an approving grunt. "I like that idea better than going back to her house. She can't accost you in a public space."

"You don't have to worry about me. She seems harmless. She was dressed in a sweater set—hardly the preferred attire of a violent criminal."

"Never trust the sweater set crowd," Kelly replies with a chortle. "*Especially* paired with pearls. Just be careful, that's all I'm saying. She's a good liar, she might have other criminal talents you don't know about."

"She's desperate to hide her true identity, that's for sure."

"You know," Kelly says, her tone unusually somber. "I'm just thinking out loud here, but do you think she might be afraid of Declan? If he's alive, he could be controlling the situation."

"I really hope you're wrong about that," I say, a knot tightening in my stomach.

"Me too," Kelly says in a grim tone. "Call me later and let me know how it goes."

Shortly before noon, I'm in surveillance mode again, watching from my vantage point as employees from the Gold Coast Auto dealership come and go through a side entrance. My chest tightens when I spot Lynelle walking out with a small group of employees. They're carrying gift bags and one of the women is clutching a fistful of helium balloons. I thump my fist on the steering wheel in frustration. I can't corner Lynelle at a birthday luncheon—I need to get her on her own. Everything is working against me and I'm rapidly running out of options. The only thing left to do is wait and catch her after work, which means changing my flight to a later one. Kelly won't be thrilled, but she'll understand.

After rebooking my return flight, I send Kelly my updated itinerary with a brief explanation.

She texts me back immediately: *Do NOT confront Lynelle at her house after dark. You can't trust her. She's been lying to everyone for years.*

I drain the last of my latte as I draft a response: *Don't worry about me. I'll be at the airport waiting for my flight well before dark.*

I while away the rest of the afternoon at a nearby mall, drinking more coffee and Googling Irish news articles on Declan's disappearance. The updates are trickling to a standstill as interest in the case continues to wane. Even the comments from trolls on my website have dried up as they move on to fresh meat. I try calling Walsh, but he doesn't pick up. I suspect he's ignoring me—tired of repeating himself. I can't blame him; there's never anything new to report. I've already provided him with dental records and everything else he requested. Now, it's a waiting game, hoping for some new lead to come in. Tonya was supposed to be helping me communicate with the Irish authorities, but her family emergency put an end to that. All indicators are that it's time for me to let go and move on, but I can't bring myself to give up on Declan. I have to find out what's happened to him.

If it turns out he's conned me out of everything Eric worked so hard for, I'll do what it takes to bring him to justice.

21

By 4:00 p.m., I'm back in Lynelle's neighborhood, parked farther down her street and tucked out of sight behind an RV. Each time someone walks by, I duck my head and pretend to be reading something on my phone as I nibble on a packet of beef jerky. Lynelle finishes work at five, which gives me plenty of time to scout out her house and figure out how best to approach her. If our first meeting was anything to go by, she won't react well if I show up on her doorstep again.

At quarter to five, I pull on the cheap beanie I picked up in town to cover my hair, don my backpack with the folder and photos, and stuff my hands in my pockets as I stroll casually down the street. When I reach 3490 Fairmount, I do a quick sweep of the surrounding area to make sure I'm not being observed, before striding up the driveway and around the side of the house. A dilapidated wooden gate blocks my entry to the back yard, but when I pull on the string dangling through the peep hole, the gate unlatches. Casting one last glance over my shoulder, I push it open, flinching when it grates over the flagstone beneath. I lift it up a couple of inches and close it behind me as quietly as I can.

My pulse races as I hurry around to the back door. It's no surprise to find it locked, but I notice a medium-sized doggie door, which sparks an idea. I tent my hands over my eyes and peer through the kitchen window. I feel a small tug of longing in my chest when I spot a caramel-colored pug curled up in a dog bed in the corner of the room. Evidently, Lynelle is a dog lover too. Maybe I can use that to get her to talk to me. I take a quick look around the yard—lined with an overgrown hedge and strewn with chew toys—and then walk around to the other side of the house where I find a dilapidated looking dog pen stacked on top of several weather-beaten storage bins. I lift the pen down and examine it. The door latch is broken but I can position it to face the side of the house so the pug can't escape. The tricky part will be luring it outside—it looks comfortable in its warm bed, and it's freezing cold out here. I pat my coat pockets and pull out what's left of the jerky I was nibbling on earlier. Food is always a sure bet. Kneeling down in front of the doggie door, I gently push the flap open. "Hey, buddy," I call out, adding a soft whistle.

The pug's ears prick up and he immediately jumps up on all fours and starts barking. I stick my hand through the flap and extend the jerky in his direction. He stares at it, dark shiny eyes bulging on either side of his flattened black face, pink tongue dangling in anticipation.

"Come on, little guy. You know you want it."

I know I've broken through his defenses the minute his tail starts wagging. Seconds later, he hurtles across the floor, skidding to a stop by my outstretched hand. He takes a tentative sniff of the jerky and then snatches it from my fingers before streaking back to his bed like a naughty child. Chuckling, I sit back on my haunches. I didn't even have a chance to lure him outside. But he'll be back. It won't take him more than two seconds to inhale that jerky. I break off another chunk and wiggle my fingers through the opening again. This time, the pug doesn't hesitate. He barrels toward me, but I snatch my fingers back before he gets a hold of the jerky. He hesitates at the doggie door, unsure of this new development in the game. I take a few steps backward and hold the jerky out to him. "Good boy. Come and get it."

In a flash, he dives through the door, and bounds toward me. I reward him with the jerky, stroking his neck as he wolfs it down. Before he can dash back inside, I block the doggie door with one of the plastic storage containers. He trots over to it and sniffs all around it, letting out a plaintive whine. To appease him, I pick up one of his chew toys and raise it in the air. "Ready? Fetch, boy!" I fling the rubber bone across the lawn, and he scampers after it, the doggie door dilemma momentarily forgotten. When he comes running back with his toy, I rub his neck and ears and praise his efforts. Then, I pick him up and carry him around to the side of the house where I place him inside the dog pen, along with his chew toy. I shove the pen up against the wall and push the remaining pieces of jerky through the wire. "Sorry, little guy. This won't be for long, I promise. I just need you to get your mama's attention for me." I leave him scarfing down the rest of my jerky and return to the back yard to suss out a good hiding spot. I end up squeezing in behind the hedge, hoping Lynelle's attention will be drawn to the side of the house by all the yapping and whining.

Minutes tick by at an agonizingly slow pace, broken up by the pug's intermittent howls. I wish I could cradle his little body to mine so we could comfort each other and keep each other warm. My ears gradually grow attuned to the sound of cars crawling down the street as residents begin arriving home. Children's voices drift through the air, the bounce of a basketball, music blaring from an open window. At last, I hear car tires crunching to a stop in the front driveway. I press myself further back against the wooden fence separating Lynelle's yard from her neighbor's. My clothes are covered in a sticky netting of cobwebs—making me thankful for the beanie preventing spiders from taking up residence in my hair. It's not long before I hear the back door opening. "Milo! I'm home! Where are you?"

The pug immediately breaks into a frenzied medley of barking, whining, and snuffling.

Lynelle steps into the yard and hurries around the side of the house. The minute she's out of sight, I slip from my hiding place and make a beeline for the back door. I scurry through the kitchen and dart into the family room. Struggling to calm my breathing, I press myself up against the wall behind the door, the straps of my backpack digging into my shoulders. My heart thumps ever more loudly in my chest as I wait for Lynelle to come back inside and close the door. I don't want neighbors overhearing her yelling at me that I'm trespassing and demanding that I leave. I don't know how she'll react when she sees me, but I need to prepare for the worst. I can't erase Kelly's warning from my mind. *She could be dangerous.* To be fair, Lynelle might be equally scared of me—I'm an intruder in her house, after all, and she has no idea what my intentions are. My eyes sweep my surroundings as I wait for her to come back inside. The decor in the family room is sparse and the furniture looks somewhat beat up. I wonder how long she's been living here. It's hard to picture Lynelle as a criminal swindling people out of their money. Still, I have every intention of staying alert and keeping my wits about me.

My breath catches in my throat when I hear her comforting Milo. "Poor baby! What were you doing in there? Did you get your toy stuck again?"

To my relief, she seems to think Milo got himself trapped. By the sound of things, it's not the first time he's got into a pickle while she was gone. I hear her rummaging around in the kitchen and then she calls, "Here you go, Milo. Din dins!" A moment later, footsteps clip across the hardwood floor in the hall and ascend the stairs. I relax my stance, wondering if I should follow her or wait for her to come back downstairs.

I'm deliberating my next move when Milo comes bounding into the room. He barks excitedly at me, tongue dangling, his wrongful imprisonment ordeal forgotten. I kneel down and rub his head. "Sorry boy," I whisper. "I'm all out of jerky. Your belly's probably full now, anyway." He scampers back out of the room and returns, a moment later, with a ragged-looking rope toy in his mouth. "I know you want to play, but that's not a good idea right now." I grab the toy and toss it into the hall, then quietly close the door on him. He barks in protest for a few minutes before abandoning the cause.

Just when I'm beginning to think Lynelle must be taking a bath, or maybe a nap, I hear her come back downstairs and go into the kitchen. I take a few shallow breaths before opening the door and padding into the kitchen, just as the microwave dings.

Lynelle spins around, the plate in her hand crashing to the floor. Her face blanches. "How ... what are you doing here?" Her eyes flit to Milo, looking up at me expectantly, tail wagging. "It was you, wasn't it?" she rasps. "You put him in the dog pen!"

Without waiting for a response, she turns and reaches for something. I take a step back, half-afraid she'll brandish a bread knife at me.

But when she wheels back around, she's holding a gun.

22

"**L**ynelle, please!" I say in a hoarse whisper, slowly raising my hands. "Put the gun down. I'm not here to hurt you."

Her eyes drill into me. "How did you find me?"

"I hired a private investigator. I knew it was you I saw at the airport terminal in Chicago."

"What do you want?"

"Can you please put the gun down and then we can talk."

She gestures with the barrel of the gun to the kitchen table. "Sit down. What's in the backpack?"

"I'll show you. I don't have a weapon." I slip the pack off my shoulder and reach for the zipper.

"Don't touch it!" she screams at me. "Toss it here."

I'm still staring down the barrel of a gun, so I do as she says. Milo bounds after the backpack, gripping it and shaking it like it's a new toy.

Lynelle lowers the gun and unzips the pack. She pulls out the folder of information from Tonya, and several photos I took from Brynn's album, before dropping the backpack to the floor. I hold my breath as she studies the photos intently without any apparent reaction. After a few minutes, she sets them on the kitchen counter, staring at me with icy indifference.

"I just want the truth," I say, picking up where I left off. "Put yourself in my shoes for a minute. My husband was abducted on our honeymoon. I paid the ransom and never heard from the kidnappers again, and then I discover his deceased first wife is still alive. Don't you think I deserve some answers?"

Lynelle cocks her head to one side. "Why? So you can go straight to the police and have me arrested?"

"I'm not interested in having you arrested. This is about me. I don't even know if I'm legally married anymore." I throw up my hands. "Or legally a widow."

Lynelle's face tightens. "I Googled the story today at work. I'm sorry for your loss, but I don't know anything about Declan's abduction. As for where that leaves you, I was declared dead, which makes you legally married."

"Why did you do it—fake your own death?"

"It doesn't concern you. I need you to leave, *now*, and this time, don't come back."

It's clear she's hiding something, but she has no intention of coming clean. I can't tell if she's working with Declan, or if she's afraid of him, like Kelly suggested. My mind thrashes about for some way to convince her to open up to me, but I'm afraid to antagonize her in case she reaches for the gun again. I gesture dejectedly at my backpack. "I need my stuff."

Lynelle gathers up the folder and photos on the counter and reaches for the backpack at her feet. Quick as a flash, Milo jumps up, tugging at the backpack like the game is back on, taking the feet out from under her. I watch in slow motion as she topples over his squat body, arms flailing as she tries in vain to recover her balance. My eyes go straight to the gun on the counter. Seizing my chance, I dash over and grab it, then swivel to face Lynelle. I stand over her, aiming the weapon at her chest, hands twitching with fear. I've never fired a gun before, let alone pointed one at a human being. But Lynelle doesn't need to know that. "Get up!" I bark.

She opens her mouth to say something but thinks better of it. Using the palms of her hands, she pushes herself up to her knees, groaning as she gets to her feet and limps over to a chair. I take a seat at the other end of the table, relieved to be able to set the gun down before it falls from my shaking hands. Lynelle can't make any sudden moves with an injured ankle, but it's reassuring to have the gun within reach of my fingertips, regardless. "Like I told you already, I'm not here to hurt you and I'm not interested in turning you in to the police. I just need to know that your double life has nothing to do with Declan's disappearance. I promise to go away and leave you in peace if you tell me the truth about why you faked your death."

Lynelle drops her gaze, squeezing her hands on the table in front of her. "I had no choice. I had gotten myself into trouble."

"What kind of trouble?"

She picks at the skin on her thumb. "I need your word that you won't tell Brynn."

I give a non-committal shrug. "I won't tell her anything that serves no purpose other than to hurt her. That's as much as I can promise you."

A resigned look settles on Lynelle's face. "I was having an affair with a colleague at the bank where I worked, a guy called TJ. We worked in the loans department together. Declan didn't know anything about it."

"I think he knew," I interrupt. "At least, he suspected as much."

She flaps a hand dismissively. "His whole life was wrapped up in his training. I thought adopting Brynn would bring us together but, although he adored her, it left even less time for us."

"Are you still with this guy?"

She twists her lips. "No. TJ's long gone. A few months into the relationship, I found out he was siphoning money from accounts. He talked me into altering some transactions to cover his tracks, but the feds were closing in on him. He was potentially facing a thirty-year prison term for bank fraud. He wanted me to go on the run with him. He said if I didn't, he would make it look like I was behind everything."

She drops her face into her hands and shakes her head. "I couldn't face the thought of going to prison for decades on end. I couldn't do that to Brynn. Much as I hated the thought of leaving her behind, I figured it would be worse for her to grow up with a mother in prison. I wasn't thinking straight at the time. I was on some heavy-duty meds for depression, and I was terrified of being caught. When I took the boat out that night, I was tempted to do it for real. In the end, TJ persuaded me to run away with him."

"And you've been hiding ever since?"

Lynelle nods. "Not that anyone's looking for me. Officially, I'm dead. I'm pretty sure TJ went to Mexico. He talked about going all the time. We were making plans to move there, but our relationship started to crumble pretty quickly after we went into hiding."

I digest the information in silence for a moment or two, trying to find holes in her story. It jives with what Declan told me about her being withdrawn and depressed—he'd even suspected she was having an affair. But the whole bank fraud story is shocking—I don't know whether to believe her or not.

"I can't keep all this from Brynn. I already told her I hired a PI to investigate you. She knows it's you in the photo."

Lynelle gives a disgruntled shake of her head. "You should have kept her in the dark. My biggest regret is what I did to my daughter."

"And what about Declan?" I ask.

"Our marriage had already unraveled by then." She throws me a pitying look. "How long did you say you were married to him?"

"He disappeared on our honeymoon." I exhale a heavy breath. "Please, Lynelle. I need the truth. Are you in contact with him?"

She stares at me, unblinking. "You think he ran off with your money, don't you?"

I shrug. "I don't want to entertain the idea, but everyone else thinks I'm being naive. You knew him. What do you think?"

"Are you asking me if Declan scammed you out of your money?"

"Yes, I suppose I am."

She gives a sharp nod. "We'd better have a drink." Pushing herself to her feet, she limps over to a small wine rack on the kitchen counter. "Red or white?"

"Either one." I stare at the gun on the table in front of me while she pours our drinks. I have a nagging feeling what little is left of my world is about to implode.

23

I fasten a wary eye on the wine glass Lynelle sets in front of me. She had her back to me while she was pouring it so I can't be certain she didn't slip something into it. I don't know her, and after the gun incident, I can't trust her.

As soon as she sits back down, she begins rambling on about her life before she went into hiding. I don't attempt to interrupt her to steer her back to my question. Now that she's talking, I don't want to cut her short in case I miss something important. I shoot Kelly a quick text letting her know I'm going to miss my flight—again—and then turn off the notifications on my phone to avoid the fallout. I'll figure out a way to make this up to her later.

"You really love him, don't you?" Lynelle says, when she's finished recounting her struggles with infertility, depression, and marital strife that led to the terrible decision she made to aid and abet in bank fraud.

"Yes, Declan's a good man."

Lynelle makes a scoffing sound. "He's too obsessed with

his marathon training to be a good husband. You didn't have enough time together to figure that out. But it's neither here nor there. You want to know if he scammed you. I can't answer the question with any degree of certainty, but I will tell you this—he was a control freak when it came to our money. It all went into an account in his name, and he doled me out a weekly allowance like I was a child. I never even knew how much he earned."

I consider this for a moment before responding. Lynelle and Declan were young when they got married. Maybe she wasn't good with money. Declan never brought up the idea of such an arrangement with me, but then I was the one with the money, and he had full access to it. It's disconcerting to hear what Lynelle has to say, and it only adds to the uneasy feeling in my gut that's been growing ever since Kelly first sowed doubts about Declan in my mind. "So you have no idea what happened to him?"

"None whatsoever. I haven't set eyes on him in years." Lynelle raises her glass to her lips and sets it back down without taking a sip. "I know you have a hard time imagining he could have staged his abduction to get his hands on your money, but you never really know someone, do you? I don't have a good track record picking guys. Sounds like Declan might be cut from the same cloth as TJ." She stares morosely into her untouched wine.

"Come back with me to LA tomorrow," I say spontaneously. "Brynn deserves to know her mother's alive. We can get to the bottom of what happened to Declan if we work together."

Lynelle traces her finger around the rim of her glass. "I can't do that. The minute word gets out I'm alive, I'll be arrested."

"No one ever connected you to the bank fraud. It's not a crime to fake your own death, is it?"

"Pseudocide—that's what they call it," Lynelle answers, a faraway look in her eyes. "It's not illegal. Believe me, I've done my research. It's everything you do after it that's illegal —triggering a false police report, living under an assumed identity, lying on government paperwork, evading taxes. Who knows what all they could get me for?"

"At least think about it. Sleep on it. You could fly back with me in the morning. We can keep it a clandestine visit if you want. You can trust Brynn to keep her mouth shut. She won't want to do anything that could harm you."

Lynelle's lips twitch into a sad smile. "I'll think about it."

I slide the gun to the middle of the table and get to my feet. "We can catch the 11:02 flight with Delta. I'll be here at 9:00 a.m. sharp to pick you up." I lean over and scratch Milo's ears as he snuffles contentedly in his bed. At my touch, he stretches his short stubby legs in the air. "And bring my new buddy," I add. "I miss having a dog in the house."

Lynelle sees me to the door, and I pull my collar up as I hurry to my car, shivering in the crisp night air.

The neighbor who returned the mop earlier peers through her kitchen window at me and abruptly pulls her blinds closed. No doubt she's even more curious about my identity now that I've spent the evening at Lynelle's house.

On the drive back to the hotel, I go over our entire conversation, combing through it for any clues or details I might have missed. Lynelle talked a lot about how depression disrupted her life. Some of her memories were fuzzy, and she got confused about details at times, backtracking on parts of her story. At one point, she broke down in tears when she recounted holding Brynn in her arms for the first time. Kelly won't approve of my decision to invite her to LA, but I can't see Lynelle participating in a racket to siphon money from widows. She seems like a broken woman. If I'm wrong, at least I'll be keeping my enemy close. The last thing I need is for her to disappear again before I get the answers I need.

As it stands, I'm still no clearer on whether or not Declan conned me and took my money. Lynelle gave him mixed reviews. I can't deny his training always came first with him, but I knew that when I married him. Maybe I wasn't as needy as Lynelle. I have a job I love, a circle of close friends, and I actually enjoy my alone time. The idea of Declan devoting hours a day to his training didn't bother me, at least not until the honeymoon. I wonder now if I would have begun to feel lonely and neglected too, after a while. I can't help but feel sorry for Lynelle despite everything she did. TJ used her and ruined her life. It's the old adage: looking for love in all the wrong places. Maybe we both were.

It's almost 10:30 p.m. by the time I get back to the hotel, but I call Kelly anyway, eager to offload everything I've learned.

"*Fi-nally!*" she answers. "I've been texting you all night. I didn't know if you were dead or alive. She could have chopped you up and boiled you on her stove by now."

"Right! How many glasses of wine have you had?"

Kelly snorts. "I'm babysitting, remember? Where are you?"

"Safely back at the hotel. Stop fluttering your false lashes and being such a drama queen. I'm fine, Lynelle's fine, everybody's fine."

Kelly sighs. "Go ahead—give me the scoop."

"Lynelle says she hasn't been in touch with Declan, and I believe her. I don't think she's involved in any kind of con with him."

"Then she'd better have had a good reason for her disappearance. Thanks to her, you're a bigamist."

"Technically, that would be Declan. But he has a certificate of death for Lynelle, which makes me legally married to him."

"I suppose Lynelle told you that too, so it must be true," Kelly grumbles. "Why did she disappear anyway?"

I fill her in on everything Lynelle relayed to me. "I know it sounds like a crazy story, but I believe her. She was so emotional when she described being out on the water that night, trying to decide if she wanted to live or die. She really thought TJ loved her until he threatened to pin everything on her if she didn't run away with him. She was on medication for depression at the time—it might have affected her decision-making."

Kelly lets out a long-suffering groan. "It's a cosmic sob story, but you have no way of knowing if it's true. Don't you think it's odd that she and TJ were involved in bank fraud and, coincidentally, you were scammed out of a million dollars—euro, whatever?"

"It's suspicious, I'll give you that. But she sounded like she was coming clean with me."

"Even if she is telling the truth, it doesn't make me feel any better," Kelly counters. "She sounds unstable."

I press my nails into my fist, remembering the gun Lynelle pointed in my face. I don't dare breathe a word about it to Kelly. She wouldn't hesitate to call the cops and have Lynelle arrested on the spot. "She's hurting. I invited her to come to LA to see Brynn. I'm going back to her house in the morning to pick her up."

I wait through a long silence on the other end of the line before Kelly responds. "You do realize if you invite her into your home, you could be an accessory to multiple crimes."

"Well, maybe I'll end up on Dr. Phil."

"It isn't funny! She could be dangerous."

"Did I mention she has a cute pug called Milo?"

"Fine," Kelly huffs. "I admit I've never heard of a pug-loving serial killer—so hopefully, she's not the first. I'm willing to hear her out, but I still don't agree with what you're doing. Have you thought about what this might do to Brynn?"

"That's the whole reason I'm trying to persuade Lynelle to come with me. Her daughter deserves the truth."

"Even if the truth means she'll be visiting her mother in prison?"

"It might not come to that. Don't mention anything to Brynn for now. I'll call her in the morning, before our flight leaves. And thanks again, Kells, for everything. I owe you big time."

I toss and turn for a couple of hours before finally falling asleep. When my alarm goes off in the morning, I groggily throw back the covers. The second I remember where I am, I scrabble for my phone, relieved to see there's no text from Lynelle bowing out. I'm tempted to call Brynn now and tell her, but I can't jinx this. I'll wait until I have her mother safely seat-belted into the airplane next to me.

After showering, I grab a quick breakfast to go in the hotel lobby before checking out. Adrenalin pumps through my system as I walk out to the parking lot. I'll be at Lynelle's place by 8:30 a.m.—a little earlier than we agreed—but she might need some last-minute persuasion.

The minute I pull onto her street, I know something is wrong. Several neighbors are standing outside their front doors, some still in their bathrobes, deep in conversation. I slow to a crawl, acid stirring in my stomach.

That's when I see the flashing lights outside Lynelle's house.

24

I pull over and park several houses down from the emergency vehicles, feeling like I might throw up. For several minutes, I sit hunched over the steering wheel in a stupor. In my heart, I know what's happened. Lynelle's finally done what she couldn't bring herself to do on the water that day. I should never have left her alone last night with the gun. I knew she was vulnerable, unstable, depressed—whatever the right word is. I chew on my lip, paralyzed by the flashing lights of the emergency vehicles. I should get out and find out for sure what's happened, but I don't trust my legs to support me. Instead, I dial Kelly's number again. "Kells, I'm outside Lynelle's house."

"Let me guess, she's bailing on coming to LA," Kelly replies, stifling a yawn.

"Listen to me. There's an ambulance in her driveway and cop cars with flashing lights parked at the curb."

"Seriously? Do you think she took ill—heart attack or something?"

My throat feels like it's closing over. "Or worse. I'm afraid she might have hurt herself."

"Why would she do that?"

"Because she doesn't trust me. She might have thought I was going to turn her in to the police now that I've blown her cover." I swallow the barbed knot of dread in my throat. "She had a gun in the house."

"What?" Kelly sputters. "How do you know that?"

I rub a hand over my brow. "Because she pulled it on me."

"Abby! I *warned* you she was dangerous."

"She had every right to defend herself. I broke into her house."

"I can't believe you kept that from me." Kelly huffs in annoyance. "What are you going to do now?"

"I'm not sure," I admit, glancing around the street. "A bunch of her neighbors are standing around outside talking. Maybe I should ask one of them what happened."

"Safer than asking the cops," Kelly agrees. "You don't want to have to explain your relationship to her to the police. As far as they're concerned, she's April Monet."

I study the hive of activity farther down the street. Kelly's right. I can't very well walk right up to the police and ask them what's going on, and I can't explain what I was doing in Lynelle's house last night without betraying her confidence. I don't even know for sure, yet, what's happened. I glance across the street at the neighbor in the house opposite Lynelle's. She's standing on her doorstep, phone pressed tight to her ear. I'm not sure if she's spotted me. She'll recognize me right away, and she's the type to ask questions. I'd rather not strike up a conversation with her. The neighbors farther down the street are a safer bet. "Kells, I'm going to try and find out what's going on. I'll call you right back."

I gather my wits about me before climbing out of the car, praying I don't collapse as I make my way up the driveway to one of the neighbors loitering in her doorway. She ends the call she was on and watches me approach, a guarded look on her face.

I try to match her expression. "What's happening at April's place? Is she all right?"

The woman glances uneasily down the street before her gaze settles back on me. "Are you a friend of hers, or a relative or something?"

"An old friend," I answer, opting for the easier lie. "I'm in town for a couple of days and we were just catching up."

The woman nods, her eyes filling with sympathy. "I'm so sorry to have to tell you ... April's dead."

I can't help staggering backward, reeling from the news, even though I feared as much. The woman reaches for my elbow to steady me. "Are you okay? Do you need to sit down for a minute?"

I shake my head, not wanting to believe it. "How? I ... I don't understand. She was fine yesterday when I saw her."

The woman twists her hands in front of her, clearly uncomfortable at being the bearer of bad news. "It was a gunshot wound to the head. The gardener found her when he arrived this morning—saw her, rather, through the window." She gives a dismal shake of her head. "It's unbelievable. Thankfully, the bus had already picked up my son for school. I wouldn't want him witnessing this."

I cover my face with my hands, my shoulders beginning to shake as the reality sinks in. She finally killed herself. *Why, Lynelle, why?* Did my visit trigger it? Am I responsible?

"Come inside for a minute," the woman says, guiding me by the elbow into her house. She takes me into the family room, and I slump into an armchair strewn with cracker crumbs and Legos. A moment later, the woman sets a mug of black coffee on the end table next to me. "I'm Darla. What's your name?"

"Abby." It slips through my lips before I can evaluate the wisdom of giving her my real name.

"This is a shock for all of us," Darla says. "To be honest, I don't even know April that well. None of us in the neighborhood did. She kept to herself. I can't imagine what you're going through as her friend."

No you can't. I don't trust myself to speak so I raise the mug to my lips, barely wetting them before shakily setting it back down. "Do you know where Milo is?"

"He's with the neighbor across the street. My son would have loved it if I'd offered to take him, but my husband's allergic to dogs."

My stomach twists at the thought of how this is going to affect Milo. Abandonment seems to be a pattern with Lynelle.

"Did you and April go to school together?" Darla asks.

I fish a tissue from my pocket and dab at my nose as I compose a benign response. "No. We were in a yoga class together."

Darla raises her brows. "Really? I had no idea she did yoga. I invited her to go walking with me, but she said she hated exercise."

I wave a hand dismissively. "It was years ago."

The doorbell rings and Darla throws me an apologetic look. "Be right back."

I hear a muffled exchange and, minutes later, she returns to the room with a swarthy, craggy-faced detective in slacks and a jacket.

"I'm Detective Shaw," he says, flashing a badge at me. "I'm sorry for your loss. One of the neighbors mentioned seeing you here last night. I understand you were a friend of the deceased."

I blink up at him, clutching my mug as I struggle to remain calm.

"She was only in town for a couple of days," Darla inter-jects. "The poor woman had no idea what happened until she pulled up here this morning."

Detective Shaw turns to Darla and offers a broad smile. "If you wouldn't mind, I could use a coffee—black, two sugars."

"Of course," she says, slipping out of the room.

Shaw turns his attention back to me. "How did you and April know each other?"

I try not to squirm under his keen gaze. My face grows warmer as I stammer a response. "I ... I didn't really know her all that well. We were in a yoga class together several years back. I was in town for a couple of days, so I thought I'd look her up."

I can't quite make out the expression on Detective Shaw's face. I have the sense he's peeling me back, layer by layer, in his mind. Maybe he can tell by my demeanor that I'm lying.

"I'll need your contact details and address."

I wet my lips and recite them off to him.

"Anyone else living at that address?" He gestures to the ring on my finger. "Your husband, I assume?"

"He's ... uh—" I cough to cover my slip. I can't reveal anything that connects me to Lynelle. She died as April Monet—as she wanted. I give a jerky nod. "My husband and my stepdaughter."

Darla pops back into the room with a mug of coffee and hands it to Shaw, hovering expectantly.

"Wonderful, thank you," Shaw says. "Could you give us a

few minutes alone? I'd like to ask Abby a couple more questions and then I'll be out of here."

"Take as long as you need," Darla says, pulling the door closed behind her. I can't help wondering if she's parked on the other side of it, eager to pick up a juicy tidbit for a neighborhood game of telephone.

"How long were you with April yesterday?" Shaw asks, pulling out a notebook.

There's no point in lying. No doubt, the hawk-eyed neighbor across the street has already told him everything. "Most of the evening. I came by after she got home from work and we opened a bottle of wine, talked about old times. I went back to my hotel around 10:30 p.m." I drop my gaze, squeezing my hands in my lap. Am I talking too much? Volunteering information is always a sign of guilt.

"How did April seem when you left?" Detective Shaw asks.

"Fine. She didn't seem depressed at all."

"Did she give any indication that she was afraid?"

I furrow my brow. "Afraid of what? She was fine when I left. I had no idea she would do something like this."

Shaw stops writing and throws me a sharp look. "Like what?"

"Kill herself." Tears spring to my eyes and I turn away. "If I'd thought for one minute she was planning on harming herself, I would never have left her alone."

Shaw slips his notebook into his pocket and fixes an astute gaze on me. "I'm afraid it wasn't suicide. April Monet was murdered last night."

25

Murdered!

The room spins around me as Detective Shaw's words slowly gel in my mind. A tingling sensation creeps up the back of my neck when it dawns on me that I won't be flying back to LA this morning, after all—maybe not this afternoon either. I'm a key witness in a murder investigation. I was the last person to see Lynelle Cafferty aka April Monet alive. I blink at Shaw, waiting on him to continue. He stares back at me, poker-faced.

"Are you sure it was ... murder?" I stammer.

"Forensics will have to confirm it, but the trajectory is next-to-impossible for a suicide. It's pretty clear someone held a gun to the back of her head."

Panic spurts through my veins as I try to make sense of it. It sounds like an execution—not a random act of violence. Did it have some connection to my visit? My thoughts circle like vultures in my brain, threatening to pick me apart entirely. Who could have done this? Is it possible TJ was involved? Lynelle said he had a violent streak—

maybe he thought she had ratted him out to me. But that would mean he's here in the States, keeping tabs on her all this time. Why would he have stayed and risked the FBI finding him? It makes no sense. I rub my thumbs in circles around my temples, welcoming the momentary release of pressure. "Was it a break-in or something?"

"I'm not at liberty to discuss the specifics of the crime scene," Detective Shaw answers. "But I would like to get some more information from you." He turns a page in his notebook, pen poised. "Were you aware that April owned a gun?"

My breath catches in my chest. *I handled that gun. My fingerprints are on it.* Surely it can't be the same one that was used to kill her. The killer would have worn gloves, unless he was brain dead. My throat feels dry as sandpaper when I swallow. I'm done for. I can barely gather enough saliva to respond. "Yes," I croak. "She showed it to me."

Shaw cocks an eyebrow. "You haven't seen your friend in years, you say you're not particularly close, and yet, she brought out her gun to show you? Did that strike you as a little unusual?"

Fear of where this conversation is heading ignites inside me, but I force myself to remain calm and think of a reasonable response. "Not at all. We were talking about how important it is as women to be able to defend ourselves nowadays. That's when she showed me her gun."

"*Showed* it to you—what exactly did that entail?"

I grimace. Shaw's like a shark, circling for blood. My mind goes back to the moment I thought Lynelle was reaching for a knife. She must have had the gun stashed somewhere on her kitchen counter. She wasn't taking any chances—she was definitely afraid of someone or something. The FBI, TJ? Or maybe it was Declan. I can't lie to the police about handling the gun. But I can't tell them I grabbed it and pointed it at Lynelle either. I might as well just hold out my wrists and let Shaw slap the cuffs on me right now. "She—April—showed me how to use her gun," I explain. "She was trying to encourage me to get one. I told her I'd survived this long with a can of mace spray, thank you very much." A shiver ripples along my shoulder blades. "I don't think I could ever bring myself to shoot someone."

Shaw's hooded eyes appraise me, revealing nothing of what's going on inside his head. "We'll need to fingerprint you to eliminate your prints."

My brain is running in circles, searching for an escape from this burgeoning nightmare. If the only prints on the gun are mine and Lynelle's, my life as I know it is over. Shaw's hunting for a killer, and I'm looking increasingly like a credible candidate.

His radio crackles and he gets to his feet. "We'll get those fingerprints taken care of as soon as I wrap up here." He strides out of the room, and a moment later, Darla hurries back in. "The detective asked if you could wait here. I told him you were welcome to stay as long as you want." She perches on the chair opposite me and eyes me curiously. "Were you able to help him with the investigation?"

I give a dejected shake of my head. "Not really. April was murdered. I'm afraid he thinks I had something to do with it."

Darla's eyes widen. "How does he know it wasn't suicide?"

"She was shot in the back of the head." I close my eyes and rub my fingertips around my aching eye sockets. The effort of holding back tears is wearing me down.

"I'm sorry. This must be awful for you," Darla says, her

face crumpling. "I'm sure you're not a suspect. The detective's only doing his job, asking questions."

"It's not that simple. April was scared of someone. She showed me a gun she'd bought for protection, and I handled it. They're saying it's the same gun the killer used. My fingerprints are on it so of course they're going to suspect me."

Judging by the look of shock on Darla's face, she's having second thoughts about hosting me in her home.

My phone vibrates in my pocket. I pull it out and glance at the screen. "It's my friend calling to check up on me," I say.

With little attempt to hide her relief, Darla jumps to her feet. "I'll give you some privacy. If you need me, I'll be outside."

I nod, knowing she can hardly wait to feed the breaking news down the line of neighbors ravenous for scandal.

"Hey, Kells," I say, pressing the phone to my ear.

"What did you find out?" she asks.

"Lynelle's dead. I can't believe this is happening. My life's falling apart in every possible way." A sob rips up my throat. "They're saying she was murdered, shot in the back of the head. I don't know how much more I can take."

"Are you serious? Was it a burglary? Please tell me she wasn't raped."

"The police didn't give too many details, but I don't think there was any sign of forced entry or sexual assault. It sounded more like an execution."

"Oh, Abby! This is horrible—after everything you've already been through. You need to get yourself to the airport and come home right now."

"I can't. The detective I spoke to wants me to go down to the station to be fingerprinted."

There's a weighty pause before Kelly responds, "I'm sure it's just standard procedure—you were in her house yesterday, after all. They need to eliminate you as a suspect. Get the next flight home when you're done, and I'll pick you up at the airport."

I lower my voice further. "Remember I told you Lynelle pulled a gun on me last night?"

"Go on," Kelly says, her tone guarded.

"I managed to get it off her and talk her down off the ledge, but it's the same gun that was used to kill her and, well ..."

My voice trails off and Kelly completes my sentence for me. "Let me guess, your fingerprints are on it." She lets out a long, low whistle. "I guess my babysitting gig just got extended."

26

"**D**o *not* go down to the police station alone," Kelly cautions me. "You know how these things go. They'll twist whatever you say and use it against you. You need to hire an attorney ASAP."

"I'll have to come clean about who April Monet really is —was," I correct myself. "That's not going to help my case. Ex-wives and current wives aren't exactly known for their spirit of sisterhood."

"Who do you think killed her?" Kelly asks. "If it wasn't random, and no one knows her real identity, that only leaves —" She breaks off, an uneasy silence hanging between us.

"Leaves whom?" I demand.

"Declan! I'm sorry, Abby, but if he and Lynelle schemed together to scam you out of your money, he could have killed her if he thought she confessed to you. You gave him the perfect opportunity to frame you when you handled Lynelle's gun. You have to at least consider the possibility that he's behind it. He's the common denominator in every-thing that's happening to you."

I frown, considering her words. The statistical probability of so many traumatic events happening to one person is slim—close to the odds of being hit by lightning twice. It's more plausible to think they're connected, and so far, the only dot connecting everything is Declan.

As much as I've tried not to go there, I can't deny the logic in Kelly's reasoning. The list of possible suspects is small. TJ had no reason to kill Lynelle, and every reason not to come back to the States.

"Think about it," Kelly urges. "It's the only scenario that makes sense. Lynelle might have called Declan after you left last night and told him you'd been there—maybe she even admitted she was considering going to see Brynn. That would have blown their cover. Declan could have come around to her house after you left to try and talk her out of it, then silenced her when she couldn't be persuaded."

I close my eyes, turning the possibility over in my mind. I don't want any of this to be real, but I feel like I'm fighting a losing battle. "What am I going to tell Brynn?"

"For now, nothing," Kelly replies. "I'll tell her you've extended your business trip for a couple of days. Now get off the phone and call an attorney before that detective comes back."

I hang up and begin Googling lawyers in the area. I have no idea if they're any good or not—I'll have to rely on online reviews. *West Coast Personal Injury, Faulk Firm Accident Attorneys, Sanger & Taylor Criminal Defense.* My finger hovers over the third name. Criminal defense is what I need, but will it make me look guilty if I lawyer up right away? I don't want to jump the gun—poor choice of pun, all things considered.

I put away my phone and wander outside to find Darla. Maybe she can recommend someone. Better still, maybe one of her neighbors is an attorney and would be willing to accompany me to the police station. I could put Maddie on the hunt for recommendations, but I'm reluctant to involve her in this mess unless I have to.

I scan up and down the street, finally spotting Darla two houses down from Lynelle's. She's standing on the lawn, arms folded, in animated conversation with an older man dressed in sweats and flip-flops. He's clutching a travel mug in one hand, waving it around as he talks. I can't bring myself to interrupt them, knowing there's a good chance they're talking about me. I'm just about to head back inside the house when Detective Shaw comes striding up the driveway. "Ready to take care of those fingerprints?"

I give a reluctant nod. "Can I take my own car?"

"Sure." Shaw scribbles down an address and hands it to me. "I'll meet you there."

Twenty minutes later, I walk into the SFPD Southside police station, bracing myself for what lies ahead. A desk sergeant takes my prints, then escorts me to Shaw's office. He gestures to the chair opposite him. "Please, take a seat."

"I thought I was done," I say. "I already submitted my prints."

"This won't take long. I just need a few minutes of your time."

Reluctantly, I sink down in the chair, my heart racing. *This is how they get you.* I should have listened to Kelly and called an attorney right away.

"April's neighbors don't seem to know her very well," Shaw begins in an amiable tone. "I was hoping you might be able to fill in a few blanks for me."

"I ... can try. Do I need a lawyer?"

Shaw raises his brows a fraction. "That's entirely up to you."

"It's just that I'm uncomfortable knowing I was the last person to see her alive and my fingerprints are on the gun. It feels like you're questioning me like a suspect."

"You're free to leave at any time," Shaw says, smiling as he taps his fingertips together in front of him. "I just have a few basic questions about April—like if she had any relatives in the area. Anything at all you can tell us that would be helpful. We need to locate her next of kin."

I pick at the hem of my sweater as I weigh his request. This is one question I can answer honestly, and it doesn't sound like he's trying to trip me up. "She doesn't have any relatives in the area. Her parents are dead and she's an only child."

Shaw makes a note of the information. "That's useful. Do you know of anyone who might have wanted to hurt her?"

I maintain eye contact, even though my stomach does a small flip at how smoothly he moved on from the basic questions he said he wanted to ask me. "No one in particular. She was nervous being a single woman living in San Francisco."

"How long have you known her?"

Two days. "A few years. We haven't seen each other in ages. Like I said, I didn't know her all that well."

Shaw kneads his knuckles on the table in front of him and nods thoughtfully. "About that. You mentioned you met at an exercise class?"

"Yes, yoga."

He rubs his hand over his jaw. "Isn't it a bit odd to look up someone you met in a yoga class years earlier?"

I shrug. "I was in town for business. I didn't know anyone else in the area. If there's nothing more I can help you with, Detective, I'd like to go home now. This has been an extremely traumatic morning and I need to get back to my stepdaughter in Los Angeles."

He gets to his feet and hands me his card. "I appreciate your cooperation. I may need to follow up with you at some point."

I give a tight nod. "Of course." I can sense his eyes boring into me as I exit the room. I concentrate on putting one foot in front of the other, half expecting to feel a heavy hand on my shoulder, and a voice telling me I'm being detained.

When I make it all the way out of the station and safely back to my rental car, I let out a shaky breath and set the GPS for the airport.

If Shaw wants to arrest me, he's going to have to come to LA to do it.

27

I land back in LA a little after 6:30 p.m. Brynn is at a volleyball game, but Kelly is waiting for me at the curb when I exit the Delta terminal. I toss my bag in the backseat and climb in, closing my eyes and exhaling in relief to be home.

"You okay?" Kelly asks, giving my hand a quick squeeze before pulling out into the traffic.

"I am now. I wasn't sure I was going to be allowed to leave San Francisco. It doesn't look good—me handling the murder weapon and all."

"You had a perfectly good explanation for why you were there, and why your fingerprints were on the gun."

I grunt. "A perfectly good *lie*, you mean."

"The police aren't idiots. They have to know you're not a murderer."

I throw her a skeptical look. "How could they possibly know that? I'm pretty sure Detective Shaw knows I'm hiding something, which means I haven't heard the last from him. He let me go, but only until he builds his case."

"That's why you need to hire a good attorney—preferably before the police get a warrant to search your house."

"I need to tell Brynn," I say with a groan. "It's better she finds out the truth from me before it comes out in the news —or worse, I'm arrested in front of her."

"It won't come to that! Why don't you try talking to Detective Hurley?" Kelly suggests. "He already knows you hired someone to track down Lynelle. It might be a good idea to bring him up to speed on what's happened and get him on your side—preempt whatever's coming down the pipeline."

I rub my forehead as I consider the idea. "You're right. If I don't get out in front of this, it only compounds the appearance of guilt on my part. I'll pay Hurley a visit in the morning. Tonight, I need to focus on Brynn. This is going to crush her. I gave her hope that her mom was alive and now it's gone forever."

Kelly sighs. "I think you should hold off on telling her until you've talked to Hurley first and hired a lawyer. You have no idea how she'll react. You know how volatile she can be. She might even accuse you of killing her mother and call the cops on you. She already blames you for her father's disappearance."

A chill crosses my shoulders. "I suppose you have a point," I say. "I'll sleep on it, but I can't put it off for long."

When we arrive at the house, the place is in darkness.

"Brynn's grabbing dinner with the team after the game," Kelly explains. "She should be back by eight. I'll fix us something to eat."

"I don't know what I would have done without you these past few days," I say. "But you don't have to cook for me. I'm sure there are things you need to take care of at your place."

She rolls her eyes. "Are you kidding me? My plants are

plastic, and I don't do pets, as you well know. I'm staying put, just in case the SWAT team breaks down the door in the middle of the night and hauls you out of here and you need my child-minding services again."

I give her a rueful grin. "If the beautician thing ever gets old, you should try a career in comedy."

She shrugs. "I have the best of both worlds. I paint people's faces *and* make them smile."

I startle at the sound of a key in the lock.

"Oh hey, Abby," Brynn says, breezing into the kitchen. "Didn't know you were coming back tonight. Kelly said your business trip got extended."

"I managed to wrap up everything today," I answer in a strained voice. "How was the game? Did you win?"

A flicker of a frown crosses her face. "Yeah. I need to get started on my homework."

She disappears up the stairs before I have a chance to say anything else.

"That's odd," I say to Kelly. "She hasn't seen me in days, and she didn't even ask if I had any updates from Walsh. First thing she usually grills me about."

"Maybe that's a good thing," Kelly says. "It's a sign she's moving on."

I stifle a yawn as I reach for my bag. "I think I'll lay down for a bit. I barely slept the past two nights."

"Go ahead," Kelly says. "I'll start on dinner."

I don't remember falling asleep, but when I wake it's light out. After brushing my teeth, I pull on my robe and head downstairs. Kelly is seated at the kitchen table scrolling through her phone, a half-drunk mug of coffee at hand.

"Where's Brynn?" I ask.

"She had early morning practice," Kelly says. "Sleep good?"

"I crashed hard. I don't think I moved all night." I pour myself a mug of coffee and sit down next to her, making a mental note to call the school later and make sure Brynn showed up for class.

"Do you want me to come with you to the station?" Kelly asks.

I give an adamant shake of my head. "You've done enough for me the past few days. I can handle it."

"And you'll line up an attorney?"

"First thing on my agenda this morning," I assure her.

Kelly empties her mug in the sink and puts it in the dishwasher. "I need to open up the salon. I'm only a phone call away if you need me."

After breakfast, I make a few calls and line up a meeting with a lawyer for this afternoon. I wish I could have had Maddie handle it—she's a pro at vetting people—but if I can keep what's happened from my work colleagues, I will. I'm already a spectacle, and I don't want to spend all day at the office dodging furtive looks as rumors fly that I knocked off Declan and his first wife. I refill my coffee and then call the school to make sure Brynn's in class.

I wait with bated breath on the other end of the line while the school receptionist checks her records. "Yes, Brynn Cafferty's here."

"Great!" I say. "She left early for volleyball practice this morning and I just wanted to make sure she was okay. She's still struggling with the whole situation with her father. She has good days and bad days."

There's a notable pause before the receptionist responds. "Mrs. Cafferty, there was no volleyball practice this morning."

I flinch as though I've been knifed in the stomach. "Are ... you sure?

"Positive. My daughter's on the team," the receptionist explains. "They've only ever had one early-morning session, and that was punishment for half the team showing up late for practice."

"Maybe I was mistaken," I say, sheepishly. "I've been gone on business for a couple of days, and I have a hard time keeping track of her schedule."

The receptionist chuckles politely. "I hear you. Anything else I can help you with?"

"No, that was it, thanks." I hang up and stare despairingly into my cold coffee. *Where are you Declan? I need you. I can't raise your daughter without you.* In the next moment, a firestorm of rage flares up inside me and before I can stop myself, I reach for the coffee mug and throw it against the wall. "I hate you, Declan Cafferty!" I scream. "I hate you for leaving me! I hate you dead or alive!" Abandoning the mess, I run upstairs and collapse on my bed, sobbing, overwhelmed, and exhausted. When I finally manage to pull myself together, I take a long, hot shower and get dressed. It's time to come clean with Detective Hurley. It will look a whole lot better for me if I tell the truth—most of it, that is —before it comes out.

HURLEY DOESN'T LOOK ALL that surprised to see me when a desk sergeant ushers me into his office. "Abby, what can I do for you?" he asks in a pleasant tone, interlocking his fingers on the desk in front of him.

I pull up a news article on my phone about the discovery of April Monet's body and pass it across the desk. "This is Lynelle Cafferty, my husband's first wife. I went to visit her a couple of days ago. The address the PA gave me was correct. She was living under an assumed identity."

Hurley glances up at me, his eyes narrowing. "Let me get this straight. You visited her a couple of days ago and now she's dead."

I nod. "She was shot shortly after I left her house."

Hurley leans back and strokes his chin. "Are you involved in the investigation?"

"I was the last one to see her alive." I squeeze the handle of my purse, hoping the lie I'm about to tell him blends seamlessly with the truth. "It gets worse. Lynelle showed me how to use the gun she kept for protection, and I handled it. Turns out it's the same gun that was used to kill her."

"Wait a minute! Stop right there!" Hurley raises his hands in front of him. "You shouldn't be telling me this without an attorney present."

"It's nothing I haven't already told the detective who's handling the case."

"I can't help you with this," Hurley says. "It's out of my jurisdiction."

"That's not why I'm here." I slide a photo of Lynelle across the table to him, along with a copy of the information Tonya provided me with. "I'm here for the same reason I came to see you the first time. I need you to find out why Lynelle Cafferty faked her death and what, if anything, she had to do with my husband's disappearance." I'm not going to tell him about TJ and the bank fraud, at least for now. I don't know if Lynelle fabricated that story or not, and I don't want to taint the investigation.

Detective Hurley leans back in his chair and rests his hands at the back of his head, staring up at the ceiling fan. "Let me get this straight. You're telling me that the woman who was shot to death a couple of nights ago in San Francisco is your husband's first wife who supposedly drowned years ago?"

"Yes! It should be easy enough to prove it was her—DNA, dental records—whatever else you use these days."

Detective Hurley eyes me sympathetically. "And you suspect she colluded with your husband to scam you out of a million euro?"

I raise my chin, my eyes trained on his. "It's not about the money. I think Declan might have killed her."

28

Seated in a chrome and felt chair in the reception area of the law offices of Hahn and Barrington later that afternoon, I take in the serene surroundings as I wait for my appointment with Sophie Hahn. Sipping on my latte, I can't help but admire the sleek, bright, modern lines of the decor—nothing like the gloomy leather and dark wood furnishings I'd expected. I'm a little early for my appointment, but I didn't feel like going into work late after meeting with Detective Hurley, and then leaving again only a couple of hours later. It was easier to tell Maddie I'm not feeling well and working from home today.

"Abby?"

I blink out of my reverie and look up at a young, smartly dressed woman in a baby blue silk blouse and gray pencil skirt. "I'm Sophie Hahn," she says, extending a slim manicured hand. Her grip is firm and cool, mirroring the poise she exudes. She flicks her long, glossy black hair over her shoulder as she leads me to her office. It's equally as minimalistic in design as the reception area, one entire wall devoted to a single print. Atop a white marble console table sits the requisite Scales of Justice statue. I grimace inwardly, remembering why I'm here. Turning my attention to Sophie, I give her a queasy grin as I take my seat. I hope she's older than she looks. I don't want to be her first test case out of college.

"I've reviewed the notes my assistant took," she begins, leafing through a notebook in front of her. "I have to say it's a tangled web. An abducted husband, a potential bigamy situation, the alleged murder of a woman who purportedly drowned, a PI gone AWOL, and then, of course, we come to your involvement which is, I assume, why you engaged my services."

"Yes," I say, setting my coffee cup down on the designated coaster on the desk in front of me. "As I mentioned to your assistant, I hired a PI to track down my husband's first wife after I spotted her in an airport terminal in Chicago. The PI found out she was living in San Francisco, and I passed the contact information, along with a surveillance photo, on to the police. Their tech team looked at it and informed me that Lynelle's face had been Photoshopped in. They weren't interested in looking into a case based on fraudulent evidence."

"So you took it upon yourself to fly up there and track her down." There's nothing judgmental about Sophie's tone, but I realize it could be another nail in my coffin from a potential juror's perspective if I'm tried for murder.

"Not with any intent to harm her," I hasten to explain. "I just needed to find out for sure if it was her. I didn't even know if I was legally married to Declan at that point."

Sophie takes a minute to jot down the information I've relayed so far. "Tell me about your meeting with Lynelle and how your fingerprints ended up on the gun."

I squirm in my seat, wrestling with how much to reveal.

Sophie sets down her pen and scrutinizes me. "You do understand we have attorney-client privilege, right? You can trust me, Abby, and it would be best if you do. I can't help you if you keep anything from me that could end up undermining any case the police might bring against you."

I reach for my coffee and take a hasty sip. "Lynelle pulled a gun on me. She wanted to know how I found her and why I was there. She was scared I was going to turn her in to the police. At one point, she set the gun down on the counter, and when her dog jumped in front of her and tripped her up, I saw my chance and lunged for the gun. I made her tell me the whole story of why she faked her death and went on the run with TJ—a guy she worked with at the bank who was wanted for fraud. They were having an affair."

Sophie taps a painted nail on the desk. "What did she tell you about TJ?"

I shrug. "She said he had a violent streak. I don't know if it's true or not. She could have been making the whole bank fraud story up."

"Why would she do that?"

I blow out a heavy breath. "I don't even want to entertain the idea, but it's possible she plotted with my husband to get their hands on my money. If that's the case, Declan might have killed her when he found out she'd been talking to me."

Sophie raises her brows. "So you think your husband's still alive?"

I shrug. "Maybe." It feels like I'm betraying Declan to admit it. My mind wanders back to when we flew into Shannon airport, fingers intertwined, euphoric at the thought of spending our honeymoon in Ireland. Our story was a second-chance fairytale—more haunted than magical as it turns out. Was Declan's love for me all an act? Was any of it real?

"Abby, did you hear me?" Sophie raises her brows questioningly.

I give a quick shake of my head to clear my thoughts. "Sorry. I missed that last part."

"I said I have everything I need from you, for now. Let me know if the police contact you and do not, under any circumstances, allow them to interview you again unless I'm present."

On the drive home, I check my phone for messages or missed calls. Between Walsh, Hurley, and Shaw, there's a good chance someone from law enforcement will be in touch before the day is out. My biggest fear is that it will be to inform me of my rights.

Twenty minutes later, I pull into my driveway and click on the garage door opener. My stomach clenches a little tighter when I see Brynn's car parked inside. I promised her Aunt Jamie I would keep a close eye on her, and I'm failing in that regard. I need to get to the bottom of why she's been lying to me, where she's going, and who she's hanging out with when she's skipping school.

"Brynn! I'm home!" I call out as I open the door.

"In the kitchen," she calls back.

She's standing over the stove flipping something in a pan when I walk in. "I'm making a grilled cheese if you want one," she says.

Even though I haven't had lunch, I'm not hungry, but it's an opportunity to talk. "Sure, thanks." I open the fridge, lift out a jug of iced tea, and pour two glasses. Brynn joins me at the table and sets a plate of food in front of me. I force myself to take a bite and chew methodically. "You make a mean grilled cheese," I say, swallowing down the congealed bread and cheese with a mouthful of tea. "How was volleyball practice?"

"Same as usual," Brynn replies, without skipping a beat.

I take another bite of my sandwich, wondering how to proceed. I feel like I'm navigating a minefield but there's no sense dancing around the issue all evening. If she's going to explode, she'll do it whether I spend five minutes smoothing the way, or five hours. I dab my mouth on a napkin and lean back in my chair. "Brynn, I need to know who you've been hanging out with lately. There is no Carrie Bleeker in your class, is there?"

She stops chewing, her eyes not meeting mine. I keep my gaze trained on her as she reaches for her glass of iced tea and takes a huge gulp.

"Are you seeing a boy?" I ask, trying not to sound accusatory. "Is that what you're hiding from me?"

Brynn wrinkles her face in disgust. "*See*-ing a boy—what does that even mean? Kids hang out or hook up nowadays."

I give a sheepish shrug. "I'm the first to admit I don't know much about teenage lingo. But you didn't answer my question. I need to be able to trust you."

She rolls her eyes, still not meeting mine. "*No*! I'm not hanging out with a boy."

I raise my palms in the air. "Fine! Then who is this Carrie Bleeker?"

Brynn shoves her plate angrily aside. "No one. It's just a dumb name I made up."

"O-kay," I say gingerly, determined to keep pushing forward. "So who have you been hanging out with when you're skipping school?"

"Friends."

I count to ten, willing patience into my tone. "And where do you and these *friends* hang out?"

Brynn picks at the crust of her grilled cheese. "People's houses."

"You're going to need to be more specific than that. Are they drug dealers or something?"

She scowls at me. "You're so not funny, Abby. Stop trying to act cool."

I let out a frustrated breath. "Then stop lying to me!"

"Why should I?" Brynn yells, her chair scraping the floor as she leaps to her feet. "You lie to me too!"

My heart begins to beat a little faster. "What are you talking about?"

"I called Maddie to ask if I could use the color copier for a school project." Brynn's eyes narrow. "She asked me if you were feeling better. She thought you were home sick today. And she didn't know anything about a business trip you supposedly went on either. So don't lecture me about lying!"

I open my mouth to respond but she's already thumping her way up the stairs. Moments later, I hear her bedroom door slam shut.

29

I stare at my iced tea, rubbing my thumb back and forth across the glass as if the action might summon a genie who could possibly put everything that's gone wrong right again. My life feels like it's turning into a puddle of quicksand. The harder I struggle, the deeper I sink. I only ever wanted to protect Brynn, but all I've done is alienate her. It will be a miracle if she comes back out of her room tonight. I can't tell her about her mother when she's this worked up. Her first counseling appointment is tomorrow, but now I'm not sure if she'll even want to go.

I try knocking on her door, an hour or so later, and she responds by cranking up her music. Any attempt at reconciliation tonight is just going to antagonize her further. I might as well turn in early and take a sleeping pill. I'm in desperate need of a good night's sleep. The only way I'm going to be able to navigate another day is if I can think clearly.

When I wake the following morning, I have a message on my phone from Walsh. As usual, he has no progress to report regarding the investigation, but he's kind enough to check up on me every so often, regardless. I'm tempted to tell him about Lynelle, but it's far too complicated a story to relay by text. Instead, I string together a generic response and hit send. Ireland already seems like a page from another life. I need to stay focused on what I have to accomplish today—namely cajoling a sullen sixteen-year-old step-daughter into a desperately needed therapy session.

When I head downstairs, I find Brynn sitting at the table buttering a blueberry bagel.

I pour myself some coffee and join her. "I'm sorry I lied. It's hard to explain but I ... had to take care of some things and I needed to do it by myself. To tell you the truth, some days I don't even want to get out of bed. I miss your dad so much it hurts." Before I can stop myself, a tear trickles down my cheek and I brush it away with the sleeve of my robe.

The expression on Brynn's face softens. She sets down her bagel and stares forlornly at it. "It sucks. Everyone else is carrying on with their lives and they don't even care. That's why I don't want to go to school. It's not because I'm hanging out with bad kids, or drinking, or doing drugs. Or anything else you might be worrying about."

"I get it, I really do, but you can't keep skipping class. You have finals coming up in a couple of weeks."

"I'll catch up. My teachers are really chill about it."

"Just don't take advantage of the situation. There's a limit to how lenient they can be."

Brynn reaches for her bagel again. "I know. As soon as I'm done with my counseling appointment, I'll talk to my homeroom teacher about getting caught up."

I duck behind my oversized coffee mug, trying not to look overly elated. "Fair enough. I'll go get ready."

The waiting area at the counselor's office is painted the color of sand, and the walls are decorated with a mixture of motivational quotes and beach scenes, mostly comprising of abstract driftwood and shell arrangements. A tabletop fountain trickles like a gurgling baby in the corner, adding to the soothing atmosphere. Brynn's counselor, Ann Russell—an older woman with a friendly face, springy curls, and gaudy, red spectacles—introduces herself and then whisks Brynn into her office. According to her references, she's had decades of experience with troubled teens, and I'm counting on her being able to penetrate Brynn's walls. Even though she assured me she's not hanging out with *bad kids*, as she dubbed it, the fact that they're cutting class and encouraging her to do the same is a red flag. There's no telling what trouble they could get into down the line, and I don't want them dragging Brynn down with them.

I look up in surprise when the door opens an hour later, and Brynn reappears. I've been lost in my thoughts and barely noticed the time slipping by. As I get to my feet, I realize she's been crying. I steal a glance at her counselor, and she gives me a tight smile. "I'll see you again next Monday at the same time," she says.

"Perfect, thank you," I say, following Brynn out to the car. She climbs in, her head drooping as she wrestles with her seatbelt.

"Are you okay?" I ask.

"I don't know," she mumbles.

"What's wrong?"

"I don't want to talk about it."

"All right," I say, starting up the car. "How did you like Ann? Were you comfortable with her?"

"She's okay," Brynn answers, turning to look out the window.

All things considered, *okay* is high praise. I decide not to press it, for now. At least she hasn't said she doesn't want to go back next Monday. Judging by her tear-streaked face, Ann was able to get her talking—it's a start.

After I drop Brynn off at school, I head into work with every intention of tackling my growing backlog of projects. To my frustration, I see Maddie has forgotten to print out some documents I requested. She has a dentist appointment this morning, so I make my way to her office and fire up her computer. I'm going to have to trawl through hundreds of emails to find the one with the attachments I need. My eyes are beginning to glaze over when I catch sight of my name. I stop scrolling and go back up to a random email from someone called Lynn Lewis—not a name I recognize.

What a crazy story! I can't believe she had enough money to pay a million-euro ransom. You're right, she must be loaded.

I click further down in the thread and read Maddie's response.

She settled the lawsuit with her late husband's partner two months ago. She was pretty tight-lipped about the details but it was bucks. Eric ran a high-end construction company. Wouldn't mind getting my hands on some of that money!

A prickling sensation spreads over my shoulders. It's uncomfortable to know Maddie has been gossiping about me in emails, but that's not what's bothering me most. I can't help remembering she called in sick the day of my wedding and was out for ten days. Was that a coincidence? I take a few, shaky breaths trying to calm myself. I can't think straight anymore. I feel like I'm about to have a panic attack.

"Morning, Abby!" Maddie chirps, as she breezes into the room.

"Oh ... hi," I stammer, whirling around to face her. "I was just looking for those spreadsheets from Hanson Engineering."

"Did I not give them to you? I know I printed them out."

Maddie frowns, her shrewd eyes sweeping the room. "Ah, here they are!" She reaches for a sheaf of papers on her credenza. "I must have set them down to grab some—" She breaks off, her gaze zeroing in on her computer screen. Her mouth forms a silent "O" and a pink tinge creeps up her cheeks.

I elevate my brows, waiting for an explanation.

"That was a personal email," she says, with a defiant tilt of her chin.

"And it was *my* personal business you were discussing," I reply. "Or should I say *wanted to get your hands on?*"

Maddie tinkles a nervous laugh. "It was only a joke. Okay, so maybe I was out of line to send the email, but I didn't talk to anyone in the office about—"

"Out of line! That's putting it mildly. You're my personal assistant. You should have known better—we deal with confidential information every day. I'm supposed to be able to trust you. Instead, I find out you've been blabbing about my settlement money to your friends. How did you even know about that? Have you been nosing around in my business?"

Maddie's eyes narrow. "No! Of course not! I overheard—"

Her voice trails off as a large shadow fills the doorway. I turn to see a familiar but unwelcome face.

Detective Shaw steps toward me, his heavy brows drawn together. "Abby Cafferty, you're under arrest for the murder of April Monet."

30

Tears needle my eyes as I walk out of jail with Kelly after posting bail. Thankfully, Sophie Hahn wasted no time getting me a hearing, which gives me some measure of assurance that she's competent. But she has a long road ahead of her to keep me out of prison. I can't believe this is my new reality. I'm supposed to be in the throes of wedded bliss, building a life with my new husband, adopting a dog together—all the things we talked about, planned for, dreamed of. Instead, I'm about to embark on the fight of my life to prove I'm innocent of murdering my missing husband's first wife—a woman I thought was dead until a couple of weeks ago. If this were pitched as a TV show, it would be considered too far-fetched to produce.

"How did Brynn take the news of my arrest?" I ask, as I plug in my seatbelt.

A troubled expression crosses Kelly's face. "She was shocked, of course. She's been acting like a frightened rabbit ever since."

"She doesn't know the murdered woman was Lynelle, does she?"

"How would she? As far as anyone knows, her name was April Monet."

"But if she looks the story up online, she'll recognize her."

"Maybe." Kelly grimaces. "I hate to be the bearer of more bad news, but the school called to say Brynn bailed on her classes again today."

I groan. "I can't really blame her. No sixteen-year-old can be expected to deal with that much trauma. I'm worried something bad is going to happen to her. I can't even come down hard on her for playing hooky—it pales in significance to me being arrested for murder."

"Those charges won't stick," Kelly says, with an emphatic shake of her head. "They have nothing on you."

"Other than the fact that I was the last person to see Lynelle alive and my fingerprints are on the murder weapon." I shudder beneath my seatbelt. "I can't think about that now. I need to figure out where Brynn's been stealing off to. I'd try putting a tracking App on her phone if I knew her passcode."

"What about an AirTag on her car?"

I slide up in my seat. "Now *that's* an idea. Can we swing by the Apple Store?"

BRYNN ARRIVES HOME SHORTLY before dinner. I suck in an icy breath as I listen for the sound of her key in the door. Kelly offered to stay but I sent her home a while ago. I need to talk to Brynn alone and find out if she's figured out the truth about April's identity. She grunts a greeting in passing and disappears up the stairs to change out of her volleyball clothes. I take the opportunity to slip into the garage and hide the AirTag under the carpet in the back of her car. When she comes back downstairs, I divvy up the chicken Alfredo pasta I've made and pour two glasses of iced tea. "You must have been shocked when you heard I'd been arrested," I say. "You know I didn't do it, don't you?"

Brynn gives a wary nod. "Was she a ... friend of yours?"

I try to swallow the piece of pasta lodged in my throat. I don't want to keep lying to her, but I don't want to break her heart either by telling her I suspect her dad of killing her mom—not until I have solid evidence. "More like an acquaintance," I reply, clearing my throat. "Kelly tells me you didn't go to school today."

Her face closes over. "It was too embarrassing. A kid in my class told everyone you'd been arrested. They were all laughing about it."

"Fair enough. But you're going to school tomorrow. You have to face it just like everything else we're dealing with. My trial could be a long process and you can't stay away from school the entire time." I get to my feet and start clearing the dishes. "I'll take you tomorrow and pick you up."

"I don't need you to drive me to school!" Brynn protests.

I shrug. "I can't trust you."

She pins a pleading gaze on me. "I promise I'll go tomorrow."

I pretend to consider it and then give a reluctant nod. If she disappears again, I'll know exactly where she's going this time. "Fine. One more chance. But I'm going to ask your teachers for a progress report at the end of the week."

I wake with a start in the middle of the night to the sound of the garage door opening. I lay in bed listening for a moment or two to make sure I'm not imagining it, and then throw back the covers and tiptoe to Brynn's room. She appears to be curled up under her duvet, but something tells me to take a closer look. My heart drops when I realize she's stuffed two pillows under the duvet. This is worse than skipping school—potentially, much worse. Good kids don't hang out at two o'clock in the morning on a school night. I race back to my room and hurriedly throw on some sweats while checking to make sure the App on my phone is tracking the AirTag. Throwing the strap of my purse over my head, I bolt down the stairs two at a time.

I drive for about forty-five minutes before my App indicates the AirTag coming to a stop at an address in Anaheim. I pull over and check the location—it's a residence in a less than desirable neighborhood. I'm guessing this is the infamous *Carrie Bleeker* whom Brynn has been hanging out with —a friend who's not in her zip code, or her school district, let alone her class. I let the car idle for a few minutes and then drive slowly past Brynn's empty car parked at the curb. I can see a light on at the back of the house indicating that someone's awake. I park further down the street and zip up my jacket as I walk back to the house, shivering in the cold night air.

After making a note of the address, I take a couple of photos, including the license plate of the red Dodge truck parked in the driveway. I'm tempted to go around the side of the house and try peeking in the window, but the last time I trespassed, I ended up becoming the prime suspect in a murder investigation. My appetite for risk has greatly diminished since posting bail. Still, I'm Brynn's guardian and no one else is looking out for her. I owe it to Declan—regardless of what he's done or hasn't done—to make sure his daughter's safe. After dithering for several minutes, I make a decision.

Tiptoeing up the driveway, I grit my teeth, half-expecting a motion-activated light to kick on and expose me. Technically, I'm not trespassing if I'm here to find a runaway minor child. But the small matter of my previous arrest history won't work in my favor. A dog barks nearby and I press myself against the wall, trying to melt into the shadows like they do in the movies. My heartbeat is thudding halfway up my throat as I try to work out if the dog can see me. It sounded close—it could be the next-door neighbor's. I wait for a good five minutes before daring to creep forward again. To my relief, the barking doesn't resume.

When I reach the back of the house, I duck down and peer over at the lit window. The curtains are pulled but there's a good three-inch gap. If I can edge my way over there, maybe I can finally learn the identity of Brynn's mysterious friend. Despite her insistence that she doesn't have a boyfriend, I'm not convinced—not when she continues to lie to me.

Whomever she's meeting, she's willing to drive a long way to see them and go to extraordinary lengths to hide their existence from me.

31

When I reach the window, I inch my head slowly upward until I can just about see through the crack in the curtains. To my frustration, the room is empty. My heart begins to beat a little faster as an unwelcome scenario springs to mind. I think of the truck in the driveway and try not to picture Brynn alone upstairs with some guy. For a fleeting moment, I consider calling the cops. But then I hear the front door slam, and the sound of a car rumbling to life. Is Brynn leaving again already? I frown, trying to wrap my head around why she would drive all the way to Anaheim and back for a twenty-minute visit? Could it have something to do with drugs? It would explain a lot of what's been going on with her, of late. I hover below the window wondering if the occupant of the house will come back into the kitchen but, a moment later, the room is plunged into darkness. Whomever Brynn was meeting has gone back to bed.

Back in my car, I crank up the heater and settle in for the drive home. Brynn has at least a five-minute head start on me. Even if I speed the whole way, I won't make it back to the house before her. The minute she pulls into the garage and sees my car is missing she'll know she's been busted. I can either admit that I followed her or lie and say I heard the garage door opening and went to look for her but couldn't find her. As I drive, I keep an eye on the location of the AirTag on my phone. Ten miles down the road, I catch a break when she pulls into a gas station. I breathe out a silent word of thanks. It should give me enough time to make it home before her. I don't want to confront her until I find out who lives at the address in Anaheim. I can't trust Brynn to tell me the truth.

Safely back in bed, I curl up beneath the duvet, tensing when I hear the garage door opening. Brynn pads up the stairs so quietly I can barely detect her movements. When her bedroom door clicks closed, I exhale and turn over, determined to try and catch a few hours of sleep before dawn.

At breakfast the following morning, the tiny pillows beneath Brynn's eyes betray her tiredness. She packs a lunch and leaves for school in plenty of time to make her first class. I keep a close eye on the AirTag's movements, relieved when I see her car pulling into the school parking lot. I set a pan on the stove to poach a couple of eggs for breakfast and turn on the television to catch the local news. I'm only half listening to the newscaster when a name catches my attention.

"Fifty-seven-year-old, Tonya Meyer, was discovered locked in the basement of an unoccupied house late yesterday afternoon when the homeowner's daughter stopped by to retrieve some personal belongings for her elderly mother."

The spatula I'm holding slips from my fingers when Tonya's face flashes up on the screen.

"We have learned that the private investigator was abducted at knifepoint leaving her office late Monday evening," the newscaster continues. "At this point, the police have no suspects. Anyone with information is asked ..."

I zone out to the rest of what she says as I dart across the floor to retrieve my phone from the charging station. My thumbs shake as I hammer out a message to Tonya.

Just saw you on the news. So glad you're safe. Please get in touch as soon as you can.

I finish making my breakfast in a daze. That explains the family emergency. Whoever abducted Tonya clearly didn't want anyone looking for her. I have a strong hunch it could have something to do with Declan's abduction, or Lynelle's death. It can't be a coincidence. I'm sure Tonya has already made the connection, although I don't expect to hear back from her right away. I wouldn't blame her if she ignores my text entirely. She's probably in shock.

I'm finishing up my breakfast when my phone vibrates on the table, making me jump. I snatch it up and read Tonya's reply.

We need to meet. This is connected to Declan. I want to help.

I rub my hands over my face, my emotions pulling me in several directions at once—relief that I won't have to rely on my own primitive investigation skills any longer, gratitude that Tonya still wants to help me, guilt that the job I hired her for almost cost her her life.

We exchange a couple of messages and agree to meet for lunch at a small café not far from Tonya's office. I get dressed and head into work, sequestering myself in my office in a bid to avoid any interaction with Maddie. I'm still angry and hurt about the email she sent, but also embarrassed at my overreaction. I realize now I was being paranoid thinking she could have had anything to do with Declan's abduction halfway around the world. I need to apologize for jumping down her throat. The last thing I need is for her to quit on me now.

At noon, I gather up my purse and keys, about to make my exit when there's a knock on the door. Maddie sticks her head inside, her face expressionless. "Got a minute?"

I give a curt nod. If she's going to tell me she's resigning, there's no point in groveling. "Better make it quick. I'm about to head out for lunch."

She slips inside the room and closes the door behind her, leaning against it in a sheepish posture. "I wanted to apologize again for sending that email. I've been churning it over in my mind ever since. It was thoughtless of me. I know you've been through a lot lately and I don't want to add to your burden by making you think you can't trust me. It was a stupid, spur-of-the-moment thing. I didn't mean anything by it, and I certainly wasn't plotting to steal your money."

My shoulders relax. "I know that. Apology accepted, and I'm sorry, too, for chewing you out. I'm hyper-sensitive right now with everything that's going on. I don't know if my husband's dead or alive, I have his angry, hurt, teenage daughter living with me, I miss Aspen, and I wish Eric hadn't died and—" My voice breaks and I take a deep breath. "I'm sorry, Maddie. I have a lot to deal with and I really need you to have my back."

"You have my word I'm there for you, whatever you need," she assures me.

I give a small nod of acknowledgement. "You've been invaluable shouldering so much responsibility and covering for me whenever I need it. Let's just label this as a silly spat and put it behind us."

A relieved smile floods Maddie's face. "Done," she says, opening the door. "Enjoy your lunch."

. . .

I DETECT a whiff of cigarette smoke when I sit down opposite Tonya in the Peasant Grill Café. Her face looks sunken, but her eyes are as sharp as ever as she appraises me.

I smile tentatively at her. "How are you doing?"

"Smoking up a storm, but no mental breakdown on the horizon," she quips.

"Did they ... hurt you?" I ask, dreading the answer as visions of a battered Declan come to mind.

"No, but they didn't feed me either. They left me with a bottle of water and no indication they were ever coming back."

I swallow down the lump in my throat at the thought of Tonya dying alone of thirst in a musty, abandoned basement on account of her connection to me. "I'd totally understand if you want to drop the case and have nothing more to do with me."

She leans across the table, her eyes never leaving mine. "That's not happening. I'm more fired up than ever to solve this—I have skin in the game now too."

"Do you think you could identify the people who kidnapped you?"

She shakes her head. "They wore balaclavas. But I'd recognize their voices—a man and a woman."

"What makes you think it had something to do with Declan?"

Tonya grabs a plastic menu from the stand on the table and passes it to me. "Order first and then we'll talk."

I select a Chinese Chicken salad and Tonya orders a bacon cheeseburger and fries. "I can use the calories," she says with a wry grin.

I clear my throat, eager to get to the heart of why we're here. "Did you overhear the kidnappers talking about Declan?"

"No, but one of them said something about Brynn. I couldn't catch what they said, but I recognized the name—it's not very common."

Blood drains from my head. "You ... don't think Brynn's in any danger, do you?"

Tonya lifts a brow. "Seems like everyone around you is a potential target. She could be next."

32

I reach for my phone with shaking fingers and check the location of the AirTag, relieved to see that Brynn's car is still in the school parking lot. She's safe, for now.

"Think about it," Tonya urges. "It can't be a coincidence that the people who kidnapped me know Brynn. This has to be connected to Declan's abduction. Maybe they thought you hired me to find them and that's why they tried to get rid of me."

I give a distracted nod. Everyone who knows me is in danger. Kelly could be next for all I know.

"They went into my office and rifled through my files," Tonya goes on. "Who knows what information they were after? If these people think you're a soft target, they might try to squeeze more money out of you, which is why I think Brynn could be their next target."

I grimace. "She might already be in danger. She snuck out last night and drove to Anaheim. She's not allowed to drive at night—she only just got her license—so I followed her."

Tonya lifts a curious brow. "How did you manage to tail her without being spotted?"

"I put an AirTag in her car."

An amused smile spreads across Tonya's lips. "If you ever consider a career change, I could use an assistant. What did you find out?"

The waitress arrives with our food, so I wait until she moves off again before answering. "She went into a house, but I have no idea who she met up with."

"Boyfriend?" Tonya suggests.

I spear some lettuce on my fork. "I don't know. I noticed a light on at the back of the place. I hung around on the street debating what to do, and by the time I'd finally plucked up the courage to sneak around and peek in the window, the room was empty. Next thing I know, the front door's closing and I hear Brynn drive off. The odd thing is, she couldn't have been there for more than fifteen or twenty minutes. Seems like the trip was hardly worth making if it was to meet a boy, but I can't imagine what else she'd be sneaking off to do in the middle of the night. I have the address, maybe you can find out who lives there."

Tonya reaches for a fry. "Shouldn't be a problem. Any other information you can give me?"

"I took pictures of the house and the license plate of the truck in the driveway." I pull up my phone and send her the photos.

"Not bad sleuthing for a first attempt," Tonya remarks, before biting into her cheeseburger. A look of intense satisfaction melts across her face as a trickle of grease oozes out from the corner of her mouth. She grabs a napkin and dabs at it. "Mmm! Mmm! You have no idea how good that tastes after two days of forced fasting."

"I can't tell you how sorry I am you got dragged into my mess."

Tonya flaps a hand at me. "Goes with the job. I miss the thrill of police work. Most of what I do is routine surveillance."

My phone beeps with an incoming message and I glance at it, a mixture of hope and dread flitting through me. "It's my lawyer," I say, setting the phone back down on the table. "She wants to schedule a meeting to go over my defense strategy. I don't know if I should come clean about April Monet's true identity. It's probably just going to seal my fate in the eyes of a jury."

Tonya fixes a steely gaze on me. "You're focusing on the wrong thing. Your court date is still two months away. I'm going to help you get to the bottom of things before that, beginning with Brynn's mysterious rendezvous in Anaheim. Give me an hour or two and I'll have that information for you."

I finish up my salad feeling somewhat reassured by Tonya's fighting words. Her abduction has only heightened her determination to get to the bottom of the tangled web of lies I find myself at the center of—culminating in indictment in a homicide.

I'm almost at Sophie Hahn's office when I get a text from Garda Walsh.

Abby, please ring me as soon as you get this message.

My breathing grows shallow as I read the text again. It's not his usual—*Give me a ring when you get a chance.* I have a feeling this isn't just another routine update. He even used my name. Was it to soften the blow he's about to deliver? Or is he excited because he's had a breakthrough? *No*—the message doesn't convey that kind of urgency. But he has something important to tell me. Maybe they've finally made an arrest. I pull into the parking lot at the law offices of Hahn and Barrington and switch off the engine. My hands are trembling as I dial Walsh's number and hit the speaker button. "It's Abby," I say, the minute he answers. I don't bother asking for an update. He knows it's always my first question.

He clears his throat before he begins. "I have some news. I wanted to call you right away before the press gets wind of it."

I hold my breath, my silence prompting him to continue.

"I'm sorry, Abby. We found Declan's body."

33

The words swirl around on a loop inside my skull. *We found Declan's body ... Declan's body ... Declan's body.* I'm vaguely aware of my fingernails pressing into the flesh of my palms, bile creeping up my throat.

"I know this isn't the outcome you were hoping for," Walsh continues, "but maybe it's some consolation knowing you can bring him home and lay him to rest now."

"Where?" I manage to croak out.

"He was in the water. A fisherman spotted something bobbing in the seaweed near the shore and alerted the Coast Guard."

"And you're sure it's ... him?"

Walsh lets out a melancholic sigh. "He was wearing running clothes. Same height, and hair color. We're waiting on the coroner to confirm it."

"We should have looked harder for him that night," I whisper. "He was probably wandering along the trail trying to find his way back."

"No sense tormenting yourself," Walsh says. "We did all we could. He might have already been in the water by the time we started looking for him. I'll know more once they've done the autopsy. Hopefully, by tomorrow."

"When can I bring him home?"

"I'll let you know as soon as his body has been released and we have a death notification certificate. The embassy will assist you in getting a transit permit."

I scrunch my eyes shut at the thought of the myriad details that need to be attended to—things I know nothing about. I'm grateful once again for Walsh's kindness. I can't think straight right now, and having someone hold my hand through the process is comforting.

"Do you have someone you can call?" Walsh asks, his tone laden with concern.

"Yes, thank you," I mumble.

"Very good. I'll be in touch again tomorrow."

I toss my phone into my purse and sit hunched over the wheel for several minutes, too stunned to react. I can't cry—maybe I don't have any tears left. I feel nothing—not even anger toward the kidnappers. I'm too numb. It doesn't seem real that Declan is dead. For the past few weeks, I've kept the hope alive inside that he would come back to me. At times, I've doubted him—wondered as others have if Declan was part of the scam—then berated myself afterward for even thinking of him that way. And now he's gone forever, his body washed up on a foreign shore like flotsam.

It hits me then that getting his body home is the least of my problems. How am I going to break this to Brynn? I groan as I rub my brow. No child should have to go through what she's suffered already. I wish I could abdicate the responsibility of having to tell her the heartbreaking news, but it falls on me as her stepmother, and her only living parent.

I straighten up in my seat and stare through the windshield at the law office in front of me. I'm officially late for my appointment with Sophie Hahn. I know she would understand if I postponed it. As I'm debating what to do, my phone rings again. When I fish it back out of my purse, Tonya's name appears on the screen.

"I have news, but you're not going to like it," she says, without preamble.

I press a hand to my chest, not sure I can take any more hits—today, or ever. "O-kay," I say, reluctantly giving her permission to continue.

"The house Brynn visited is rented by a woman named Angel Lotze. The truck is registered to her live-in boyfriend, Mick Foster. Ring any bells?"

"No."

"They both have rap sheets. I'll send over their mugshots when I get back to my computer. It appears Brynn's been hanging out with some pretty unsavory characters."

I chew on my lip, letting her words sink in. "How unsavory?"

Tonya lets out a heavy sigh. "We're talking robbery and kidnapping."

34

I send Sophie a quick text to reschedule our appointment, and then message Kelly.

They found Declan's body. Can you meet me at my house?

Kelly's already waiting at my front door when I get home. I collapse into her arms, sobbing as she escorts me inside. She plants me at the kitchen table while she fixes me a strong coffee.

"Are they sure it's Declan?" she asks, handing me a steaming mug before taking a seat next to me.

"They identified his running clothes, same hair color—who else could it be?" I wipe the back of my hand over my eyes. "Walsh said he'll call me as soon as they have the autopsy results."

"Where did they find him?"

A shiver ripples over my shoulders as I cradle the mug in my hands. "A fisherman spotted him in the water."

Kelly frowns. "He drowned?"

"I don't know," I say, biting back more tears. "If he slipped and fell from the cliff top, he would have been dead before he hit the water." I let out a soft sigh. "I can't believe he's gone. Maybe now everyone will stop trying to convince me Declan was in on his own abduction."

Kelly reaches over and gives my hand a quick squeeze. "I'm sorry, Abby. You shouldn't have to go through losing your husband again—especially not like this."

"As hard as it is, I'm more afraid of what this is going to do to Brynn."

"I don't think it's going to come as a big surprise. She had to have known it was unlikely her dad was still alive. At least now she has closure."

"She's going to flip out when I tell her," I say. "Our relationship is already so strained. She's still lying to me. She snuck out last night and drove all the way to a house in Anaheim. I had Tonya do a little investigating and it turns out the couple who live there are criminals—Angel Lotze and Mick Foster. They did time for robbery and kidnapping."

Kelly stares at me, her mouth hanging open. "How on earth does Brynn know these people?"

"I have no idea. But if these are the same people who were involved in Tonya's kidnapping—possibly even Declan's—then Brynn might be their next target. She has no idea of the danger she's in. Tonya thinks they might try and use her to extort more money out of me."

"And you don't know who they are?"

"I don't recognize the names, but that doesn't mean anything. If Lynelle managed to figure out how to live under an assumed identity, I have no doubt a criminal could do it. Tonya's going to send over their mugshots when she gets back to the office."

Kelly pulls out a gloss and applies it to her lips, looking thoughtful. "They must have lured Brynn with something."

I frown into my mug of coffee. "She does have a new iPhone. She was very cagey when I asked her about it—I was afraid she might have stolen it, but they could have given it to her. You never know what they could be grooming her to do. I just don't know how she got tangled up with them to begin with. Declan never mentioned her sneaking out or hanging out with anyone suspicious. It must have begun when we went to Ireland on our honeymoon—Jamie caught her in a few lies when she stayed at her house."

"I don't know about the whole grooming thing," Kelly says, sounding dubious. "Maybe Brynn's hanging out with this couple's kid or something."

I shoot her a startled look. "I never thought of that. Tonya didn't mention anything about kids, but I can ask her when she sends the mugshots over." I glance at the time. I still have an hour or so before Brynn's due home. "I'm going to call Brynn's counselor and see if she can fit her in for a session tomorrow. She'll need someone to talk to about her father's death, and I doubt she'll want to open up to me."

Kelly gets to her feet. "I'll see what you have in the fridge for dinner."

After I dial the counseling practice and explain the situation to Ann, she graciously clears her schedule and arranges for an emergency consultation with Brynn the following morning.

When I hear the sound of a car pulling into the driveway, I throw Kelly a loaded look.

"Want me to make myself scarce while you tell her?" she asks.

"No, stay," I say, grabbing her by the sleeve. "She likes you, and I might need your words of wisdom if it doesn't go well."

I take a deep breath, counting Brynn's footsteps as she walks down the hallway and into the kitchen.

"What are you two up to?" she asks, tossing her backpack in her usual spot on the floor and heading straight to the refrigerator. She helps herself to a water and joins us at the table.

I wet my parched lips as I turn to face her. "Brynn, I have something to tell you. I got a call from Ireland today."

Her eyes flick to Kelly and back to me. "What is it? Have they found Dad?"

I wilt inside at the note of hope in her voice—hope that I'm about to crush with a sledgehammer. "I'm so sorry, honey. They've found his body."

Her eyes pool with confusion, and then narrow. "I don't believe you! You're lying!"

I grimace. "I know it's heartbreaking to hear. I didn't want to believe it myself either. It won't sink in for a while that he's gone."

Brynn gives a defiant shake of her head. "That's not possible! I know Dad's not dead."

I rally what little will I have left to continue the conversation. Exhaustion is overwhelming me—physical, emotional, mental. It feels like I'm wading through mud that is rapidly caking on my legs and dragging me down with every step.

"It's scary to think that your dad's gone," Kelly says softly. "It's okay to be mad, or sad, or whatever else you feel right now."

"Shut up, Kelly! Just shut up!" Brynn explodes. "You're not part of my family." She whips her head around and glares at me. "Who told you Dad was dead?"

"Garda Walsh. A fisherman found his body near the shore."

"I don't believe it!" Brynn says. "It couldn't have been Dad. Prove it!"

I wince, knowing how much she's hurting. I understand her need to reject the awful reality she's facing—to deny the pain is real. The journey through grief is one I'm all too familiar with. "They identified your dad's clothing. They're doing an autopsy to confirm it's him. I realize this is extremely painful, Brynn, and you probably feel lost and alone, but I want you to know that we're all here for you; me, Kelly, your Aunt Jamie—even your counselor. She's rearranged her schedule to see you first thing in the morning."

"Nobody's here for me! Nobody *ever* is!" Brynn yells. "That's the whole problem!" She leaps up from the table, knocking her chair to the floor, and runs from the room.

"Brynn! Wait! Please!" I call out.

"Leave her. Give her some time," Kelly says, laying a hand on my arm.

Defeated, I sink back down in my chair. "I don't know how to help her. I thought she would burst into tears or something, but she seems more angry than anything."

"She's a teenager," Kelly says. "Her emotions are all over the place. The tears will come when she's ready. Even if she doesn't want to talk to us, at least she has that counseling appointment in the morning."

I give a dubious nod. "Hopefully, she'll open up to Ann. She cried at her last appointment, so I know Ann's getting through to her."

Kelly and I spend the evening reminiscing about Declan and looking through wedding photos—pictures I haven't even had a chance to frame. Brynn refuses to come down for dinner, and I respect her wishes to have some time to herself.

After Kelly cleans up the kitchen and heads home, I turn in for the night, but it's hours later before I fall into a fitful sleep. My mind is too busy trying to stitch together all the pieces and figure out how they connect.

When I wake the following morning, there's another message from Walsh.

Autopsy complete. Please ring at first chance.

I sit bolt upright in bed and dial his number. "Hi, it's Abby."

"I suppose you're just waking up," Garda Walsh replies in his usual kindly tone. "Did you get any sleep?"

"A little. Is it ... him?"

"It is. The coroner confirmed it thanks to the dental records you sent over. I'm very sorry for your loss."

"How ... did he die?" I squeeze my eyes shut as I wait for his answer. I want him to tell me it was instantaneous the second he hit the water. It would be a horrible kind of irony if it turned out that Declan had drowned. They say it's a dreadful way to die, and I can't bear to imagine his lungs filling up with cold, Atlantic water so far from home.

"He was dead before he fell, Abby. He was beaten to death."

35

"Are they sure that's how he died?" I ask.

"His injuries are consistent with a severe beating," Walsh answers. "Broken ribs, punctured lung, internal bleeding. There was no water in his lungs, which confirms he didn't drown. We believe the kidnappers tossed his body off the cliffs, then told you they'd released him in the trailhead parking lot."

I scrunch my eyes shut trying to dull the image of Declan's body falling like a rag doll head over heels hundreds of feet to the Atlantic ocean below. There's a certain mercy in knowing he was already dead and didn't experience the sheer terror of being tossed from that height. I can't imagine a more frightening way to leave this world. But it doesn't lessen my anger at everything he underwent at the hands of the thugs who killed him.

"We'll be adding a murder charge to the legal complaints already filed," Walsh says.

I don't bother responding. I know the odds of ever catching the kidnappers—murderers—is slim and dwindling by the day. They're probably soaking up the sun on some foreign beach by now.

After I hang up with Walsh, I make my way downstairs and traipse into the kitchen in a haze of shock. The autopsy has only confirmed what I already knew, but will Brynn accept it? She was in complete denial when I told her Declan's body had been recovered. It's more critical than ever that I get her to her counseling appointment this morning. I can't help her navigate this trauma alone—I can barely cope myself. I brew some coffee, welcoming the familiar robotic activity to occupy my mind. When I'm on my second cup, I go back upstairs and knock on Brynn's door to make sure she's up.

"Brynn, are you awake? We have to leave for your appointment soon."

She thumps her way down the stairs at the last possible minute to avoid having to converse with me. After grabbing a banana from the fruit bowl, she follows me out to the car, a scowl carved into her face. I make a couple of attempts to engage her in conversation, but she shuts me down. Now's not the right time to tell her Walsh has confirmed what she least wants to hear.

In the waiting room at the counselor's office, Brynn sits hunched over her phone, her thumbs in constant motion on her screen. I'm sitting opposite her so I can't see what she's up to. Best case scenario, she's playing a game, but I have a sneaking suspicion she's communicating with whomever she snuck out of the house to meet the night before last—Angel, Mick, or possibly their kid?

"Morning Brynn, morning Abby," Ann greets us, in her usual upbeat manner.

"If I could just have a quick word with you before the session," I say, promptly getting to my feet.

"Of course," she answers, graciously ushering me inside her office with a wave of a garishly manicured hand. "We'll be just a minute, Brynn."

She glances up disinterestedly, then shrugs.

The door clicks closed, and I sink down in the couch opposite Ann.

"How can I help you?" she asks.

"As I told you yesterday, Brynn's refusing to accept that they've found her father's body. Just this morning I got word that the autopsy confirmed he was beaten to death. I haven't shared that with her yet. I wanted to get your advice on how best to approach it." I hesitate, searching for the right words. "Actually, I was hoping you might be able to break the news to her in the session this morning. She's barely speaking to me. She might accept it if it came from you."

Ann flashes me a sympathetic smile. "I can only imagine how overwhelming this is for you, trying to deal with your own grief as well as that of a teenage stepdaughter who resents you. I'll do everything I can to support you both and guide you through this process, but it would be more appropriate if Brynn heard this directly from you. How about you tell her while I'm in the room—that way I can help her work through her emotions?"

"Thank you, that would be helpful," I say with a certain measure of relief. Overall, I recognize it's the best solution. I won't look like a total coward for delegating the task to a stranger, and I'll have the support of a professional to handle Brynn's unpredictable response.

"The other thing you should know," I continue, "is that she snuck out of the house again last night and drove to a residence in Anaheim. I haven't confronted Brynn about it, yet, but she's putting herself in danger. The occupants both have rap sheets. I don't know if she went there to meet a boy, or if she was buying drugs, or what."

Ann adjusts her red spectacles, looking somber. "I'll talk to her about it. You understand I'm a mandatory reporter?"

I nod. "Do whatever you need to do to keep her safe."

Ann rises to her feet. "Wait here. I'll fetch her."

I steel myself for the conversation ahead as she opens the door and invites Brynn to join us.

She tromps into the room, throwing me a sour look before slumping down in a cushioned seat. "I don't want to talk with *her* here. You said our sessions were confidential."

Ann gives an understanding smile. "We'll have a chance to talk in private in just a minute. Abby has something to tell you before we begin, and I felt it would be good if we discussed it with all three of us in the room."

Brynn's features darken. She folds her arms in front of her and slides farther down in her seat.

Ann opens a small notebook in her lap and gives me a nod.

I squeeze my sweating hands in my lap and turn to face Brynn. "Garda Walsh called again this morning. They've completed the autopsy and confirmed it was your dad's body that was recovered."

I pause, allowing Brynn the chance to respond, or react in some way. She keeps her head hung low, not meeting my eyes or Ann's.

"Brynn, do you understand what Abby is saying?" Ann asks. "I know it's hard to accept that your dad is dead. Death is not a concept we can easily come to terms with—it takes time."

Brynn stares at her sneakers. "Did my dad *drown* too?" She spits the word out with such venom that I'm taken aback for a moment. I don't know for sure what's going through her head, but it's hardly surprising she's mistrustful of anything she's being told. If her mother faked her death, why not her father too?

Ann catches my eye and raises her brows, inviting me to respond.

"No, he didn't drown," I say. "He was badly beaten by the kidnappers. He died of his injuries."

Brynn's head jerks up. She stares at me, wide-eyed, the look of confusion on her face quickly morphing into one of horror. She opens her mouth to speak, but her bottom lip begins to tremble.

"I'm sorry, honey," I say, rising from my seat to comfort her. She shrinks back from me, and Ann signals for me to sit back down.

"I know this is very difficult to hear and you're probably feeling a lot of different emotions right now," Ann interjects. "Do you have any questions for Abby?"

Brynn's shoulders heave up and down as she chokes out the words, "I ... hate ... her!"

Ann turns to me. "Abby, why don't you step out and let Brynn and I finish our session now."

I reach for my purse and return to the waiting room, dejected and drained. That went about as well as I expected. Thankfully, Brynn's in good hands with Ann. I send Kelly a quick text to update her on the situation and then call Maddie. "No crises this morning, I trust?"

"Everything's under control," she assures me.

"Any mail?"

I hear shuffling on the other end of the line. "Just routine stuff I can process and file for you. There's one that looks personal. No return address. I'll leave it on your desk for you."

I frown. "Go ahead and open it. I want to know what it is."

I tap my foot impatiently, listening to the sound of Maddie ripping open the envelope.

"Well?" I prompt.

There's a beat of silence before she answers, "It's a type-written note: *Have your PI back off or I'll blow the lid off April Monet's true identity.*"

36

"Who's April Mon—" Maddie's voice trails off. "Sorry," she mumbles. "I didn't connect the dots, at first. Any idea who sent this?"

My stomach twists. "Probably just some troll getting off on the news about the murder."

"That's sick!" Maddie says. "Do people have nothing better to do with their lives? Want me to toss it?"

"No. Save it—it's evidence of harassment. Don't tell anyone else about this. I need your discretion, Maddie. The last thing I want is for the press to get wind of the note. I should be there within the hour—I'm at Brynn's counseling session right now." I hang up and immediately call Tonya to tell her about the threatening note. "I'm afraid for your safety. It might be in your best interest if you drop my case."

Tonya snorts. "Right when things are getting interesting —not a chance! Don't worry, I know how to protect myself. But I'd like to take a look at that note before you turn it over to the police."

"I have no intention of turning it over to them," I say. "They'll ask too many questions. If they figure out who April

Monet really is, they'll definitely put me away for murder. I can drop the note by your office after—" I cut the conversation short when the door to Ann's office suddenly bursts open and Brynn storms out. "Call you back," I mumble to Tonya, as I jump to my feet. "Brynn! What's wrong?"

She tries to push past me, but I reach for her elbow. "Wait! Your session's only half over. You can't just charge out of here."

Ann scurries over to us. "Brynn, let's sit back down and talk about this.

"I don't want to talk about *her*," Brynn yells, glaring at me, her eyes glittering with tears.

"I can help you work this out," Ann says. "Your stepmother's the only parent you have left."

"No, she's not!" Brynn retorts, tears rolling down her cheeks. "My mother's alive!"

My heart sinks at her words. I'm the one who fed her hope. Now, I'm going to have to be the one to break it to her that her mother's dead. She hasn't connected the dots, yet, that April Monet is Lynelle Cafferty. As if she doesn't hate me enough already. I lock eyes with Ann, and she gives me a tight smile. As far as she knows, Brynn's mother drowned years ago. She must think the poor girl's losing it.

"Why don't we all go back inside my office and discuss this calmly?" Ann suggests. Without waiting for a response, she guides a shaking Brynn inside, and I follow behind.

"Let's resume where we left off, shall we?" Ann begins. "Remember we were talking about grief being a process? It's going to take time, Brynn, but you will get through the tragic loss of your father. You'll move through the stages of grief just like you did when your mom died." Ann pauses, drawing her brows together in concentration. "Sometimes fresh trauma can make us regress."

"My mother's not dead!" Brynn insists, brushing the tears from her cheek with the back of her hand.

My pulse throbs in my throat. How can I tell her the truth without incriminating myself? She doesn't know that I found Lynelle Cafferty living under an assumed identity. I can't tell her who April Monet was, but it's not fair to let her cling to the false hope that her mother's alive anymore either. I have to compromise on the truth to spare her any more pain. "I ... thought I saw her at the airport," I stammer, "but I might have been mistaken."

Brynn narrows her eyes at me. "I'm not talking about her."

"I don't understand," I say, smoothing a hand over my brow.

"I'm talking about my birth mother," Brynn snaps.

I glance at Ann, but it's clear from the expression on her face that she's equally blindsided.

Brynn tilts her chin up. "I found her through ancestry.com."

My mouth drops open. I have so many questions I don't know where to begin. I throw Ann a beseeching look, grateful when she intercedes. "Have you been in contact with your mother?"

Brynn drops her gaze. "I sent her a message on Facebook."

"When was this?" I ask, finally finding my voice.

"When Dad told me he was getting married."

I do a quick calculation in my head. She's been in touch with her biological mother for the past eight months. How is it possible Declan never suspected a thing? "Is this who you snuck out of the house to visit the other night?"

Brynn jerks her head up. "How do you know about—" She breaks off and gives a sheepish nod. "Yes."

"Well, this is wonderful news," Ann says, beaming. "And now that it's out in the open, I'm sure Abby will be supportive of your relationship with your biological mother. You won't have to sneak around anymore to meet with her."

My phone dings with a message, and I glance down at it. My breath hitches in my throat when I see the mugshot Tonya has sent me. Angel Lotze is the spitting image of Brynn—an older, craggier version.

And I suspect, a far more dangerous version.

37

Ann spends the last few minutes of the session coaching us on how to navigate this new relationship with Brynn's biological mother. Neither Brynn nor I say much, other than to respond to Ann's prompts. I'm too busy obsessing over how much information Brynn has fed her mother during the past eight months, and if Angel Lotze and Mick Foster could have been behind the abductions. Tonya said her kidnappers were a man and a woman, but it's a stretch to think they flew to Ireland and abducted Declan, too.

When our session ends, Ann escorts us to the door. "I'll see you both next week. I'm happy to include Brynn's biological mother in any of our future sessions, if you feel that would be helpful."

I try not to hide my revulsion as I thank her and beat a hasty retreat.

Back in the car, Brynn and I sit side-by-side staring through the windshield, the loaded silence between us growing heavier by the minute. There's so much I need to ask her, but I'm not sure where to begin. I start with the obvious. "Why didn't you tell your dad that you'd found your bio mom?"

She doesn't say anything at first, so I repeat the question, trying not to sound accusatory.

"I was mad at him for marrying you," she blurts out. "When I found Angel, I wanted it to be my secret. She said he wouldn't let me see her if he knew. That's why I had to sneak out every time."

"You should have told me instead of lying to me for the past few weeks."

"Angel warned me not to," Brynn replies. "She said you'd be jealous and put an end to it."

I throw up my hands. "So why are you telling me now?"

Brynn fidgets with her hair. "Because I'm afraid."

"Of what?"

"Of Mick—her boyfriend." She casts an anguished look my way. "He's dangerous."

A chill inches its way up my spine. "What makes you say that? Did he hurt you?"

"No, but I overheard him talking with Angel about needing to teach that scumbag PI a lesson."

"Did you hear him say anything else that made you uneasy?"

She furrows her brow. "He always asked a lot of questions about you and Dad. He wanted to know about the settlement money you got. And Angel was always going on about how hard she's had it and how she wished she could land a windfall like that. I got this weird feeling about it. I mean, I don't think they had anything to do with what happened to Dad but—"

She breaks down and I reach over and lay a hand on her shoulder. "It's okay."

"No, it's not! I should have told you sooner. I'm so sorry."

"You're doing the right thing by telling me now." I smooth a hand over her tousled hair as another thought occurs to me. "Brynn, did you tell Angel and Mick that I saw Lynelle at the airport?"

Her face crumples. "Angel wanted to know everything about my life. I told her you'd hired a private investigator to find out if my adoptive mom was alive. I showed her the photo Tonya gave you and she gave it to Mick to see if he could find her on Facebook. Angel said you'd hired the PI to follow me, and that would lead her to them. She was afraid the PI would cause trouble for her and Mick. They've been in trouble with the law before. She said they wrote some bad checks." Brynn lets out a gut-wrenching sob. "I'm afraid they might have kidnapped Tonya."

I grimace as it all begins to come together. I have a feeling I know exactly what Mick was doing with that photo of Lynelle. He probably edited it to cast aspersions on Tonya's work, and when that didn't suffice, he abducted her so she couldn't expose him. I bet he was behind that note warning me to make my PI back off too.

My heart begins to race a little faster. What if Mick was behind Declan's abduction? "We have to go to the police with what we know."

Brynn picks at a ragged fingernail, a woebegone look on her face. "What will happen to me?"

"Nothing," I assure her, as I start up the car. "You're a minor—you were taken advantage of. Angel pumped you for information and used it for nefarious purposes. I'm sorry, but your biological mom is not a good person. Writing bad checks is only the tip of the iceberg."

Brynn blinks across at me, tears glimmering in her eyes once more.

My heart is crushed for her. Every adult in her life seems

to fold and disappear in a puff of smoke. I'm the only one left standing. It falls to me to do whatever I can to protect her. And part of that includes telling her the truth about April Monet.

I take a deep breath. "There's something else you need to know. Remember when I lied and told you I was going to San Francisco on business and Kelly stayed at the house with you?"

She nods, fixing a curious gaze on me.

"The truth is there was no business trip. I went to look up the address Tonya gave me for your mother. It was her— Lynelle Cafferty. She'd been living as April Monet for years."

I watch as a dizzying array of emotions move across Brynn's features. She blinks back tears, her brow trenched. "But that means ... Mom faked her own death. Why would she do that? Why did she leave me and Dad?"

I recoil from the pain in her voice. It almost makes me want to lie to her again to protect her, but it's time she knew the truth. "She regretted leaving you, but she felt trapped. She was having an affair with a colleague at the bank where she worked. He had committed bank fraud and she helped cover his tracks. She went on the run with him to evade the authorities."

Brynn buries her face in her hands. "All this time I blamed Dad. I thought he was the reason they didn't love each other anymore. Mom always complained that he loved running more than her. I thought it was his fault she'd gone out on the boat that day and drowned—or pretended to. Now, I've lost both of them." She lifts her head and looks directly at me, wiping at her tear-streaked face with the back of her hand. "I know you didn't kill her. Do you think Mick did?"

"It's possible. He might have followed me there."

She buckles her seatbelt, a desolate look on her face. "Let's go right to the station. I'll tell the police everything I know."

I give a somber nod as I put the car in gear and pull out of the parking lot. Time is of the essence. If Angel and Mick have killed before, they won't hesitate to do it again.

When we arrive at the police station, I ask for Detective Hurley. "Please tell him it's urgent. I have information about an ongoing investigation."

We don't have to wait long before we're ushered into his office. "Good to see you both again," he says. "Have the police in Ireland made an arrest yet?"

"No, but the charges have been upped to include murder," I say. "My husband's body was discovered a couple of days ago by a local fisherman."

Hurley rubs a hand slowly over his jaw. "I'm very sorry to hear that. My condolences to you both."

"Thank you, we're still trying to absorb the shock, although that's not why we're here this morning. We wanted to talk to you about something else."

Hurley frowns. "You understand I can't discuss the murder charge against you."

"This is about a different crime that was committed in your jurisdiction. I believe I know who abducted Tonya Meyer."

Hurley hefts an interested brow.

I gesture to Brynn. "My stepdaughter has something you might want to hear."

I give her arm a reassuring squeeze. "Go ahead."

She begins in a faltering tone but quickly gathers steam as she details Angel's and Mick's conversation about the PI, and their thirst for details about my settlement money. "At first, I was happy my biological mom was interested in my life," Brynn says. "I enjoyed all the attention. But now I have a bad feeling about it."

Hurley clasps his hands in front of him, pinning her with his gaze. "When exactly did you get this *bad feeling* as you put it?"

Brynn shrugs. "I'm not sure."

"In the past couple of days, perhaps?" Hurley prompts.

A flicker of unease crosses Brynn's face. "Maybe. I mean, when the autopsy results came back and confirmed that Dad had been murdered, I was worried they might have had something to do with it." Her voice wobbles. "I don't know how they could have, but—"

"This is very traumatic for her," I say throwing Hurley a chiding look.

He ignores me, fixing his full attention on Brynn. "You know what I think? I think you knew all along that Angel and Mick were planning to abduct your Dad to shake him down for money. And you were okay with it as long as that was as far as it went. But he wasn't supposed to die, was he? That's why you're here."

38

I suck in a sharp breath, horror-struck by Hurley's accusation. Blood pounds in my eardrums when I see the guilt contorting Brynn's face.

She ducks her head, tears sliding down her cheeks. "They were only supposed to scare him. I ... wanted to ... p-punish him for marrying Abby. I didn't know about the ransom. I never meant for ... It's my fault he's dead!" She succumbs to her sobs, wrapping her arms around her head as if to hide from the awful truth.

Hurley gets to his feet. "I need to get a unit over there right away and bring Angel and Mick in for questioning. What's the address?"

I pull out my phone and give him the information, along with Mick's license plate number. "I'll be back momentarily," he says, striding out of the office.

"What's going to happen to me?" Brynn asks, when her sobs subside.

I can't hold her searching gaze. Part of me wants to put an arm around her and draw her close, but another part of me recoils from the very thought of touching her. She's a better actress than I could have imagined. I'm reeling from the realization that if it hadn't been for her, Declan would still be alive. She fed the monsters who killed him with all the information they needed. I can't fault her for wanting to bond with her biological mother, but she crossed a line when she hid their relationship from her dad. She had to have known it was wrong.

"Nothing's going to happen to you," I say, the words ringing hollow. The truth is, she's in a precarious situation. She might need a lawyer. I'm about to text Sophie Hahn and ask for her advice when Detective Hurley reappears. "We're working on bringing them in. I'll contact Tonya Meyer and ask her to meet us here. If she can identify their voices, we'll be able to hold them and get a search warrant for their residence."

"So, what happens now?" I ask. "Are we free to go?"

Hurley turns to Brynn. "Once you give a written statement, you're free to leave. As long as you cooperate fully with the investigation, we won't be pressing obstruction charges."

BACK AT THE HOUSE, I call Kelly and summarize the latest developments.

"I'm coming over with food," she insists. "Chinese or pizza?"

"Mo-Shu Shrimp sounds good to me," I say, "and Brynn loves Chicken Chop Suey."

"I'm on it. See you shortly."

After checking in with Maddie at the office to make sure no more threatening notes have turned up, I call my lawyer.

"It sounds as if the police are offering Brynn immunity in return for her cooperation," Sophie says. "The fact that she's only sixteen works in her favor. However, there are too many unknowns at this point. I'd recommend retaining a lawyer to protect her interests. As you're aware, I can't represent her as long as I'm representing you. I'll have my assistant text you a couple of references. Now, let's talk about April Monet."

I let out a weighty sigh. "I told Brynn who April was. I think my best chance to clear my name is to come clean with the police too. There's a possibility Angel Lotze and Mick Foster were behind Lynelle's murder, but if I don't come clean, the police won't make that connection."

"I agree it's the best course of action," Sophie responds. "I'll accompany you to the station tomorrow to give your statement. I'll have my assistant text you a time once I confirm it with Detective Hurley."

I pass the remainder of the afternoon catching up on emails and finalizing arrangements regarding the transport of Declan's body back to the United States. I've been trying to plan a memorial service, but I'm finding it next to impossible. I feel as though I'm grasping at straws when I try to write down my thoughts. It was different when Eric died. We were high school sweethearts—the finish-each-other's-sentences kind of couple. It seems like I knew my first husband forever. In contrast, Declan and I were still in the getting-to-know-each-other phase. It's not as if I can stand up in front of our friends and families and talk about the memories we shared over the years. The things we did have in common are taboo subjects—the tragic demise of our first spouses, a resentful daughter, a honeymoon turned murder investigation.

I'm tempted to scrap the whole idea of a memorial service and just have a private burial instead. The circumstances of Declan's death will make it difficult for everyone in attendance. There are no words for such an occasion, and I'm not sure I can stomach spending an afternoon listening to people talking about how shocking it all was. Their shock is a pinprick compared to the pain I'll endure for the rest of my life.

When the doorbell rings shortly before six, I close my laptop with a sense of relief. Laden down with bags of delicious smelling Chinese food, Kelly heads straight to the kitchen, while I run upstairs and knock on Brynn's door. "Kelly's brought dinner."

"I'm not hungry."

"You need to eat something. It's your favorite—Chicken Chop Suey."

"I have to finish my homework. Can you put mine in the fridge for later?"

I sigh as I make my way back downstairs. Maybe she just needs some time to decompress—it's been a very long, draining, and difficult day.

Kelly ladles our food onto paper plates while I pour two glasses of iced tea. As we eat, I update her on everything that's transpired.

"I need to keep a close eye on Brynn for the next couple of days," I say. "Detective Hurley was pretty hard on her, and she has a lot of remorse for her role in all of this. I doubt she'd harm herself, but I don't know for sure."

Kelly nods thoughtfully as she chews on a mouthful of food. "She must feel awful. Do you want me to try and coax her down to eat?"

"She wants to finish her homework first. If she doesn't come down soon, I'll send you up to work your charm on her."

My phone buzzes and Detective Hurley's name comes

up on the screen. I set down my fork and hit the speaker button. "Abby speaking."

"I'm afraid I have bad news. Angel and Mick have packed up and disappeared."

Goosebumps prickle along the back of my neck. They must have found out we were talking to the police, which means they've been following us. "Are we in any danger? What happens now?"

"They're considered fugitives from justice. We're doing everything in our power to find them. In the meantime, I'll assign a squad car to patrol your neighborhood." Hurley ends the call promising to contact me again first thing in the morning.

I lock eyes with Kelly and give a distraught shake of my head. "I can't believe they got away—I know they had something to do with Declan's death. He won't be able to rest in peace until they're found."

Kelly frowns, tapping her manicured nails on the table. "Forget resting in peace. Are you going to be able to *sleep* in peace?"

I shrug. "Hurley said they'll be patrolling the neighborhood. I doubt Angel and Mick will risk showing their faces here."

"It's not them I'm worried about." She leans across the table and lowers her voice. "Brynn knows more than she's letting on. You need to watch your back."

39

I barely sleep that night after Kelly plants the seeds of doubt in my head about Brynn. Her bombshell suspicion came out of left field, but it's been eating at me ever since. Could Brynn have been in on it from the beginning? It seems preposterous to think she would go along with a plan to take her father hostage for a million euro, but so far everything about this situation has the makings of a TV true crime show. After tossing restlessly for an hour or two, I climb out of bed and lean a chair beneath my door handle. If nothing else, it will alert me if someone comes for me next.

I've already made up my mind to search Brynn's room as soon as she leaves for school. I've never invaded her privacy before, and I don't relish the thought of doing it now, but Kelly sold me on the idea. "Think about all the lies she's told you," she whispered to me over dinner last night. "You don't know what else she could be hiding from you."

"Like what?"

"I don't know, an older boyfriend, drugs, plans to run away—it could be literally anything. She hasn't exactly earned your trust, has she? The last thing you need is to find out she's been doing something illegal right under your nose. It's not as if biohazard mom and her Mickie-the-loser boyfriend have been a great influence on her, and she's on thin ice with the law. You're the adult and she's living in your house. You need to take charge of the situation."

I can't argue with Kelly's logic. It falls on me to make sure Brynn has no more surprises up her sleeve.

When I hear her moving around downstairs the following morning, I drag myself out of bed and join her in the kitchen. I'm shocked at how bedraggled she looks, her skin unusually pale, her dull eyes hung with bags.

"You must be starving," I say. "You never came down for dinner last night."

She shrugs. "I fell asleep. I'll take mine for lunch."

I open the fridge and set the cartons out on the counter. "Brynn, you can't blame yourself for what happened to your dad. It's not your fault."

She reaches for her backpack, brushing past me as she exits the room. "I don't want to talk about it."

I sigh as I replace the cartons of congealed food in the refrigerator. She's shutting me out again, and I can't tell if it's because she's hurting, or manipulating me.

As soon as I hear her car pull out of the garage, I head upstairs and watch from my bedroom window to make sure she drives off before I go into her room. My eyes sweep the space, uncertain of what I'm looking for. Everything here is new and pristine: the French country bedspread, faux sheepskin rugs, soft white slip covered armchair, fringed blue and peach cushions, gray wallpaper flecked with over-sized pink and white roses—Declan's and my lavish attempt to make Brynn feel wanted and loved in our new home together. I press my lips tightly together at the sting of tears. It didn't exactly work like a charm.

Determined to accomplish what I'm here to do, I pull my shoulders back and scan the room, trying to decide where to begin. My eyes land on the overflowing desk. I pad across the soft pile carpet and begin rummaging through the drawers, taking care to leave everything the way I find it. There's nothing of note—thankfully, nothing illegal either. My eyes drift toward the bathroom, the more likely place to stash a secret horde of pills, or drugs, or anything else Brynn doesn't want me to find. I step inside and open the mirrored cabinet above the sink. After rooting around in her toiletries for a few minutes, I find nothing of consequence other than a bottle of Motrin and some cough syrup—hardly enough to get high on. I search around the back of the toilet and even lift the lid off the tank to make sure there are no plastic bags of drugs lurking in strange places.

Satisfied that Brynn isn't hiding anything in her bathroom, I return to the bedroom and slide open the drawer in her bedside table. I rifle through the contents; a fantasy book she's reading, some birthday cards, a handful of coins, empty candy wrappers, and miscellaneous hair accessories. I slam the drawer closed and cast another glance around the room. Perhaps Kelly's fears that Brynn is hiding other secrets from me are unfounded, but now that I've violated her private space, I intend to do a thorough search. I walk over to the slipcovered armchair in the corner and pat all around it, feeling somewhat foolish for frisking a chair. I peek under the seat cushion and then turn my attention to the bed. Kneeling next to it, I slip my hand beneath the mattress and feel my way along the entire length of it. I'm about to get back to my feet when my fingers bump up against something. I shove my arm further under the mattress and grab hold of what feels like canvas material. I pull it out and stare at the tote bag in my hand, a strange fluttering in my chest. Do I really want to know what's inside and why Brynn is hiding it under her mattress?

I sink down in the armchair and clutch the bag to my chest, tracing the outline of the contents with my fingers. It feels like a book. It could be perfectly innocent—a photo album or mementos of her adoptive mother, perhaps. Private memories not intended for my eyes. On the other hand, it could be something related to Angel and Mick— evidence of their crimes. It's up to me to protect Brynn if they've exposed her to anything illegal. Before I can talk myself out of it, I tip the bag upside down and let the contents slide into my lap. It's a teal journal with silver accents adorning the padded front cover.

An uneasy mix of anticipation and dread bubbles inside me like water coming to a slow boil. I remove a bobby pin from my hair and insert the round end into the lock, jiggling and twisting the pin until I hear the welcome click of the lock popping open. Guilt ripples through my gut once more at the thought of delving into my stepdaughter's most private thoughts. Getting to my feet, I take a quick peek through the window to make sure there's no sign of her returning unexpectedly. Reassured that all is clear, I resume my seat and open the journal at a random page.

I told Dad I don't want to go to Aunt Jamie's next weekend but of course he won't listen. He never does. He's too infatuated with Abby. He's taking her skiing which is dumb because she doesn't even know how to ski.

I flip through several more pages, passing over the usual teenage ramblings and rants about friends, boys, and teachers, only stopping when I see my name pop up from time to time. The recurring theme of resentment is hurtful, but unsurprising. From the outset, Brynn made no attempt to hide her displeasure about her dad's plan to remarry. I flick halfheartedly through the remainder of the pages until I get to the final entry.

Angel will tell the cops I gave her the idea. They won't believe her of course—a convicted criminal. They should. I really hate Mick. He didn't keep his promise. And now Dad's dead. All that's left for me is the rest of Abby's money. It will be mine one day. I hope I can wait that long.

I clamp a hand to my mouth, shaking as I reread the words. *I hope I can wait that long.* What's that supposed to mean? Am I next? It sounds ominous but maybe I'm reading too much into it. Teenage girls write outrageous things in their journals all the time.

Kelly was right about one thing, though. Brynn was in on everything from the beginning—she tracked her bio mom down, messaged her on Facebook, told her about my money, planted the idea in her head of how to get her hands on it, and even went along with her own father's abduction to punish him for marrying me.

I pick at the skin around my thumb, wondering what to do with the incriminating information in the journal. I could use it to nail Brynn as an accessory to murder, but I can't find it in my heart to do that to her. She was devastated by Lynelle's death and hurt by her father's marriage to me. I can understand why she set out to find her bio mom. All she ever wanted was to be loved. I've done my best in that regard, and I'm committed to doing what I can to protect her —she's Declan's daughter, after all.

I frown down at the flowery script spilling over the pages in the journal. On the other hand, she's also Angel's child. I'm not sure what all she's capable of. I'm going to have to watch my back so I don't end up another statistic—one of those unlucky people who randomly fall out of windows or trip down flights of stairs.

I flip through the remainder of the empty pages in the journal, startled when a folded sheet of paper floats to the floor. Opening it, I find myself looking at a bank statement. My eyes widen in disbelief at the opening deposit of $100,000. I quickly scan the transactions, of which there are only three: a Lululemon purchase, an Amazon order, and another online order for the Apple store. Almost immediately, Brynn's new iPhone comes to mind. My pulse slows to a dull thud as my eyes travel slowly up the page to the account holder's name at the top.

Carrie Bleeker.

40

It's just a dumb name I made up.

Another thing Brynn lied about. I sink to my knees on the soft carpet trying to piece it together. Why does she have Carrie Bleeker's bank statement hidden under her mattress? When I first noticed Brynn's new phone, I was afraid she might have pinched it from a kid at school, or possibly shoplifted it. But this is worse—so much worse. If she's stealing from Carrie's bank account—potentially $100,000 dollars—she's going to be in serious trouble with the law, regardless of her age.

I bite down on my lip until it begins to bleed. I dab frantically at it with a tissue. What should I do? What would Declan want me to do? He'd be devastated at Brynn's deception, but he would try to protect her, at all costs. If I was on the fence about getting her a lawyer before, I'm not anymore.

I pull out my phone and leave a message with Sophie Hahn's assistant requesting an urgent appointment. Hopefully, one of her associates can see us today. I'll pull Brynn out of school early if I have to. I fold the bank statement back up and slip it between the pages of the journal. That's when I notice a small pocket on the inside cover. Peeking inside, I spot a driver's license. My heart thumps a little harder. It can't be Brynn's—she drove her car to school this morning. Swallowing back the sick feeling in my throat, I slide the license out and stare at the photo of a serious-looking, bespectacled young woman in a blonde wig. My skin crawls when I realize I'm looking at Brynn. My eyes travel over the fraudulent details on the card: eighteen years old, lives in Anaheim, *Carrie Bleeker.*

I gasp in horror, my brain abuzz with static. Angel and Mick must have helped her acquire a fraudulent identity so she could open a bank account and hide the money from Declan and me. This is proof positive that Brynn was in on the scheme from the beginning. She knew all about the ransom and was even given some of the money—presumably to buy her silence. But then it all went wrong. Declan was never supposed to die. He was supposed to come home with me once I paid up. No wonder Brynn blames herself for her dad's death. She must be freaking out inside—unable to talk to anyone about it, including her counselor—without incriminating herself.

I have to confront her about what she's done. She needs to understand the seriousness of the situation. But I'll reassure her that I'll help her. I'll get her all the counseling and legal help she needs. Despite what she's done, I don't want her blaming herself for Declan's death. She's a hurt child who was manipulated by a pair of money-grubbing criminals.

I take the canvas bag containing the journal downstairs and set it in plain view on the kitchen table. The minute Brynn returns home from school, she'll know the game is up.

I've just sat down with my laptop to tackle some work when Sophie Hahn calls me. "I got your message. I hope nothing's changed regarding the police pressing charges against Brynn."

"Everything's changed," I groan, unable to keep the despair out of my voice. "I found something in Brynn's room that links her to her father's abduction. She opened a bank account with a $100,000 deposit under an assumed name."

"Don't say another word," Sophie cautions. "Can you bring her in this afternoon at four to meet my associate, Clive Barrington?"

"Thank you. We'll be there," I say relief flooding through me. I hang up and rub my aching shoulders. I wish I didn't have to go through all this alone. I wish Declan was here. But if he were, I wouldn't be going through this anyway because none of it would have happened. I blink back tears, trying to keep my thoughts from spiraling into despair. The truth is, I'm not alone. I have Ann's and Sophie's professional counsel to lean on, and Kelly's always there at a moment's notice when I need her. I slump into a chair at the table and pull out my phone to text her. I can't tell her what Brynn said about getting her hands on my money. Knowing Kelly, she'll freak out thinking I might be suffocated in my sleep or something.

You were right to be wary. I found Brynn's journal and a fake ID she used to open a bank account.

Kelly's response is instantaneous.

What??? Did you call the police?

I hesitate before responding. She won't understand why I'm more focused on trying to help Brynn than protecting myself.

Not yet. Meeting with a lawyer this afternoon.

Good! Keep me posted. I'll bring dinner and sleep over tonight. xoxo

I send her a smiley face emoji in response and then get up to fix myself a sandwich. I have no real appetite but I'm lightheaded and I should eat something. I need to have my wits about me to face Brynn when she returns home from school—passing out from low blood sugar won't help either of us.

When I hear her car pull into the garage, I straighten up and go over in my mind what I need to say to her. I set my phone to record and slip it into my pocket. I don't want her twisting my words later in case this goes downhill.

Brynn tromps into the kitchen, her eyes immediately lighting on the canvas bag on the table. When she looks at me, I hold her gaze, my silence demanding an explanation. I can almost see the gears whirring inside her brain as she weighs her options—grovel for forgiveness or deny everything? Her face flushes and I brace myself for an outburst.

"How dare you go through my stuff!" she yells. "My room's off-limits. We agreed I would have privacy in this house, and you violated it!"

"You lost the privilege of privacy when you lied to me," I respond more calmly than I feel inside. "As it turns out, it's a good thing I went through your things." I gesture at the bag. "I found the bank statement. I don't think you have any idea how serious this is, Brynn."

"Stop treating me like a child. My dad's dead. Is that serious enough for you? Do you really think I wanted that? I didn't kill him. I didn't kill anyone, unlike *you*." Her eyes flash and she takes a step toward me. "If you hadn't gone hunting down my adoptive mom, she'd still be alive. Her blood's on your head. Try living with that!"

"No," I say, shaking my head. "I won't let you put that on

me. If you hadn't gone along with everything Angel and Mick proposed, Lynelle would be alive today. You and I both know they're the ones who killed her."

Brynn glares at me. "They wouldn't have had to if you hadn't butted into our lives."

"Why did you go along with it, Brynn? Was it for the money?"

"That's all you think about, your stupid money!" she screams. "You don't care about me. No one does. Angel didn't want me when I was born. Lynelle pretended she did, but she wanted TJ more. And Dad only loved me when I didn't come between him and his stupid running. And then *you* came along, and he had even less time for me. I *hate* you!"

I raise my hands in an attempt to soothe her. "Okay, calm down and let's discuss this. What you've done is fraud and you're going to need a lawyer. I know you don't want me helping you, but your dad's not here—I'm all you've got."

Brynn glowers at me, her whole body shaking. "You don't get it, do you? It should have been *you*!" she screams, thumping a fist on the table so hard I jump. "They were supposed to abduct you. I wanted to hurt Dad by scaring you. Angel said they'd give me some money for my trouble, but I didn't know they were going to demand a ransom. But you know what—I'm glad they took it! I hate you for ruining my life!"

"I'm still going to help you," I say, forcing calm into my voice. "I made an appointment with my lawyer's partner at 4:00 p.m. He's probably going to advise you to turn yourself into the police so we can get this sorted out. It will look better if you come clean now, rather than waiting for this all to come out at trial—and it will. Once Angel and Mick are caught, they're not going to protect you. They'll be desperate for a plea deal, and they won't hesitate to throw you under the bus."

"I'm not going to any lawyer and you're not going to show this to anyone," Brynn shouts, snatching the canvas bag from the table.

I jump up and wrestle it back from her. "You can't run from this anymore! We're going to do the right thing from now on, or I'm calling the cops to come pick you up."

Brynn stares at me for a long minute, her eyes wild with rage. "Fine!" she huffs, at length, before marching over to the refrigerator.

I let out a relieved sigh and sink down in my chair. "We can get through this, one step at a time."

"Yeah, right. Arm-in-arm, like we're buddies." Brynn slams the refrigerator door shut and turns toward me, a bizarre smile spreading across her face. "You think you can control me, don't you? You and your stupid phoenix circle of love. You don't even know me." She raises her right arm, and I catch the glint of a blade. Terror grips me when I realize she's holding my carving knife. Everything begins to move in slow motion before my eyes, then, suddenly, she's lunging at me. I scramble to my feet in an effort to dodge the blow, but I don't move quickly enough and she catches me on the shoulder, slicing into my skin.

Shock discharges in my brain. "Brynn! What are you doing?" I scream, clutching my shoulder as searing pain radiates through it. I turn my trembling palm over and show her the blood on my hand. "You cut me! What are you thinking? Put the knife down!"

I stare at her, expecting her to be overcome by remorse at what she's done. To my horror, she smirks and steps toward me.

She isn't finished, yet.

41

The look on Brynn's face is cold as ice, her eyes glittering with unchecked fury. Fear claws its way up my chest as she takes another step in my direction. It's clear she intends to finish what she started. She must be having some kind of psychotic episode. I don't want to hurt her, but I have to do something to defend myself. My gaze veers left and right, all the while keeping her in my range of vision. There's nothing within reach other than the wooden chair I was sitting in. Gritting my teeth against the pain in my shoulder, I grab the chair and hoist it above my head. When she lunges at me again, I smash it down on top of her. She shrieks and takes a faltering step backward but doesn't fall.

"Stop it, Brynn!" I call to her in a strangled voice. "This isn't you! You're not thinking straight!"

"I'm gonna kill you," she growls, the tiny flare of her nostrils giving credence to the rage fermenting inside her. Advancing once more, she raises her arm to hack at me with the bloody kitchen knife. My pulse roars in my ears as I will myself to fight for my life. I slam the chair into her, this time connecting with her wrist. She screams long and hard, the sound piercing through my head as the knife goes clattering across the tile floor. Dropping to her knees, she howls like a wounded animal. Judging by the way she's holding her wrist, I'm guessing it's broken. A wave of guilt threatens to sidetrack me, but my brain screams at me to move. I dart around the table and kick the knife into the hall before dialing 911. Through ragged breaths, I recount the incident to the dispatch officer, one eye fixed on Brynn the entire time to makes sure she doesn't make any sudden moves.

When I'm done, I text Kelly, bawling like a baby when she messages back that she's on her way. Reassured that help is imminent, I hover in the kitchen doorway, keeping my distance from Brynn who's still on the floor, nursing her wrist as she rocks back and forth.

"You broke my arm! You're a monster!" she wails. "Call an ambulance!"

"I already did." I don't bother telling her that the police are on their way as well. I'm afraid she might try to run, injured or not. Much as I want to believe that Brynn lashed out at me in a moment of rage, the look in her eye told me she fully intended to kill me. If I don't file a police report, she might try and turn the tables on me and tell them I attacked her first.

Relief seeps through me when I see flashing lights outside. I sprint to the front door and yank it open. A stocky officer steps forward, gun drawn, followed by a cluster of police and paramedics.

"Is the suspect armed?" he asks.

I shake my head, adrenaline draining from me. "Not anymore. She's on the kitchen floor."

I follow the officers inside and sink down on a chair at the table, feeling woozy as police and paramedics swarm the room, bagging evidence and barking into radios. One of the medics begins dressing my wound while two more attend to Brynn who is alternately sobbing and moaning. "My step-mother attacked me. She broke my arm! I was only trying to defend myself."

"Abby! Are you all right?" Kelly cries, rushing into the room.

I nod, biting back tears, not wanting to say too much in Brynn's earshot. The innocuous canvas bag containing evidence of more of her crimes is still lying on the table. I surreptitiously slide it onto a chair out of sight. I'm not about to open that Pandora's box, right now. She's in enough trouble as it is.

Once Brynn has been wheeled out on a gurney to a waiting ambulance, I pull out my phone and pass it to the officer in charge. "I recorded everything. You can play it back."

He listens to the entire episode intently, his expression grave. "You had a narrow escape. Your stepdaughter won't be able to circumvent an attempted manslaughter charge, at a minimum. I'm placing her under arrest as soon as she's discharged from the hospital."

I nod unhappily, knowing it's the inevitable outcome. "I'll call her lawyer." I'm still on the fence about whether or not to bring up the fraudulent bank account. It's my money in there, so it's not as if I'm contributing to someone else's suffering by hiding it. It feels like I would be betraying Declan by piling more charges on his daughter in her darkest moment.

I decline the paramedics' offer of an ambulance ride to the ER and enlist Kelly to drive me instead. I'll need stitches but, thankfully, it's a relatively superficial wound and didn't go through to the muscle.

"Do you want some water?" Kelly asks, peering anxiously across at me as I recline in the passenger seat and close my eyes.

"No, I'm good. Just a little dizzy."

"You're lucky to be alive. I can't believe she came at you with a kitchen knife."

"She's messed up from all she's gone through," I say, feeling the need to defend her.

"Lots of kids are messed up," Kelly shoots back. "They don't all try to slash their stepmothers' throats."

"I'm not making excuses for her. I turned her in, didn't I?"

Kelly eyes me reprovingly. "What about the fake ID and the bank account she opened? Did you tell the police about that?"

"Not yet. I need to think it through first."

"What's there to think about? There are consequences for what she's done—it's time she faced them."

I turn to stare out the window. "The bank account links her to Declan's murder. She didn't intend for him to die—"

"That's right, Abby—she thought it would be *you*!" Kelly fumes.

"She was angry when she said that—she didn't mean it. Facing an attempted manslaughter charge will shake her up enough. If I turn everything over to the police, they might decide to try her as an adult. Do you really think that's what she needs—to spend years in prison learning from hardened criminals? She's hurting! She needs therapy!"

We pull into the hospital parking lot and Kelly switches off the engine. "It's your call, Abby, but don't ask me to babysit again if she's released to your custody with an ankle monitor. You might be willing to risk your life, but I'm not risking mine."

· · ·

AFTER THE ER doctor stitches me up and discharges me, Kelly drives me home. "Sure you don't want me to sleep over?" she offers.

I shake my head. "I'm fine. I'm just going to take some Ibuprofen and go to bed."

I lie awake for hours wrestling with what the right thing to do is. Do I owe it to society to make sure Brynn pays in full for everything she did? Or do I owe it to Declan to shield his daughter from the brunt of Angel's manipulation? I made a commitment at our wedding ceremony to look out for her. All the adults in her life have failed her in one capacity or another—maybe a little grace and mercy would serve her well, for once. An attempted manslaughter charge might be enough to bring her to her senses, without the added baggage of being tried as an accomplice in her own father's murder.

When I wake the following morning, I replace the canvas bag beneath Brynn's mattress. I have no peace at the thought of exposing its contents.

42

The following day, Clive Barrington calls to let me know that Brynn has been transferred to a youth detention facility to await trial. "The judge isn't willing to release her back into your care at this time due to the violent nature of the crime," he explains.

I exhale a silent breath. I can't say I'm not relieved. "How's she doing?"

"She understands the gravity of the situation and she's accepted the judge's decision. She gave me a list of things she wanted you to bring her, but as I made clear to her, she'll only be allowed to bring her own tennis shoes—all other items will be provided by the facility. I'll email you the address. I can meet you there this afternoon at three if you like. I need to go over a few things with both of you." He hesitates for a moment. "If you prefer not to see her, I can make other arrangements."

"I'll be there," I say, rolling my injured shoulder. It's a little stiff but I should be fine to drive. Thankfully, I'm not on any heavy-duty painkillers. Kelly would take me if I asked her, but there's really no need—not when the lawyer will be there to serve as a buffer. I'm not sure Brynn will want to talk to me alone.

I spend the next half hour or so searching for the tennis shoes Brynn requested. Eventually, I find them at the bottom of a gym bag in her closet. I have no idea how she's going to survive in the youth facility without her designer clothes, extensive makeup collection and iPhone, but other kids make it through without losing their marbles. She'll learn to cope. I throw a quick glance at her bed as I exit the room. I still haven't made up my mind what to do about the bank account. I need to discuss that with her lawyer in private. I don't want to do anything that could come back to bite either of us from a legal standpoint.

The juvenile detention facility is a little over an hour's drive away. My shoulder throbs if I use my arm too much, so I'll have to allow myself some extra time in case I need to pull over and rest. After gathering up my things, I head out to the garage and toss Brynn's tennis shoes in the backseat. Hopefully, they'll serve as a stark reminder of everything she's going to have to give up for the foreseeable future thanks to the choices she made. I turn on the car ignition and hit the garage door opener, fumbling to connect my phone to Apple Airplay.

Suddenly, the passenger door is wrenched open. My muscles lock in fear when a woman jumps into the seat and slams the door. I open my mouth to speak but freeze when a cold circle of steel presses against my T-shirt. Dark eyes glare at me from under the brim of a gray twill cotton baseball cap. My brain fills with static. "You can take my money. Please don't hurt me."

The woman makes a scoffing sound. "Things are a little more complicated now."

My eyes widen in recognition as my throat slowly closes over. "You're ... Angel, Brynn's mother."

She cocks an eyebrow—plucked to an unnatural crescent shape. "Thanks for the introduction. Now drive."

"Where ... where are we going?"

"Just shut up and drive before you start attracting unwanted attention. Do exactly what I tell you and no one needs to get hurt. Deviate from my orders and someone else in your circle dies. Might be that arrogant PI you hired, or your beautician buddy who likes to stick her nose in your business."

"I'll do whatever you want. Leave them out of this. They have nothing to do with any of it," I say, backing the car slowly out of the garage. Between the fear pulsing through me, and my aching shoulder, I'm inching onto the road like a ninety-year-old with cataracts.

"Take a left at the end of the street," Angel barks.

A jogger with headphones and a Doberman on a leash run toward us, and Angel presses the barrel harder into my side. "Put on your best-day-ever face and smile," she hisses through the pseudo smile on her own face.

I give a jerky wave to the jogger in passing, hoping he'll detect a coded cry for help in my strained expression, but he doesn't even look at me.

I follow Angel's directions in silence for several minutes, trying to figure out how best to extricate myself safely from the situation. I don't know what her intentions are, but I've got a feeling it's about more money—enough to disappear across the border with. She knows the game's up now that Brynn's been arrested.

"Get on the 5 north," Angel says, consulting her phone.

I shoot her a questioning look. "Why? Where are we going?"

She ignores me, awkwardly typing a one-fingered message into her phone while keeping the gun trained on me.

"Are you messaging Mick?" I ask.

"If you must know, I'm giving him our ETA."

"You don't have to do what he tells you. You could turn yourself in and work out a plea deal."

"If you know what's good for you, you'll shut your mouth, and drive," Angel says, sounding bored.

A sick feeling swirls around in my gut. Whatever chance I have of getting away from Angel, I have no chance against both of them. I have to come up with a plan before we get to wherever it is Mick is holed up. "So what's our ETA?"

"That's on a need-to-know basis," Angel snaps.

"I do need to know. I need to use the restroom."

"You just left the house."

"I forgot to go before I left, and now I'm nervous which makes me need to go more."

"Suck it up!"

"Can't we stop at a gas station and I'll run in real quick?"

Angel rolls her eyes. "Why don't I just give you the gun while we're at it?"

"I'm serious. If you don't let me stop, I'm going to pee on the seat and that's what you'll be smelling for the rest of the trip."

Angel slams her fist down hard on the dash. "Enough with the jabbering! Pull over at the next rest stop."

She glares across at me, her eyes full of loathing. She doesn't see me as a person—I'm a liability that has to be handled. I fall silent once more, not wanting to aggravate her now that I've managed to talk her into making a pit stop. Ten miles down the road, I finally spot a sign for a rest area.

"Pull off and I'll scope it out," Angel orders me.

I put on my blinker and take the exit, slowing to a crawl as we approach the parking lot.

"No! Too many vehicles," Angel mutters. "Keep driving. Get back on the freeway."

"But I really—" I yelp in pain when she suddenly smashes the gun against my hip bone.

"Drive!" she roars.

"Okay! Take it easy! I'll keep going." Panic surges through me as I merge with the freeway traffic once more. I have no idea how much longer this trip is going to take. I could have five hours left, or ten minutes. Whatever I do, I have to make a move while I'm alone in the car with Angel.

If we reach Mick, I'm dead.

43

We drive for another fifteen minutes or so with Angel intermittently directing me to speed up and slow down. For the most part she instructs me to stay in the slow lane and not draw attention to ourselves. I eye each exit longingly as we pass, asking myself if she would really pull the trigger if I tried to thwart her plan. If she shoots me at the wheel, she'd be risking her own life too. I guess there's only one way to find out. I take a few shallow breaths, mustering my courage when I see a sign for the next exit two miles ahead. The steering wheel is slick with sweat beneath my grip, and my shoulder throbs from the pressure of holding on too tightly.

Just when I've psyched myself up to make a move, I spot a police car up ahead. My pulse ratchets up a notch. I'm too far away to signal for help. If only there was some way to telepathically relay my predicament. I slacken my death grip on the steering wheel, second guessing my decision to veer off the freeway at the next opportunity.

Angel slides up in her seat on full alert the minute she

spots the squad car. "Stay in this lane behind the semi-trailer," she mutters urgently.

"Okay," I say, alternately stretching my fingers and gripping the wheel as I hastily try to come up with a plan. Moments later, Angel's phone beeps with an incoming message. The second she glances down at it, I jerk the wheel and swing out into the fast lane, narrowly missing clipping a silver BMW Coupe. The irritated driver sits on his horn.

"Hey! What are you doing?" Angel screams, whacking me on the side of the head with the gun. "Get back in the other lane!"

I grit my teeth against the pain as I floor the gas, weaving in and out of vehicles like a mad woman. I race past the police vehicle, delirious with relief when the welcome sound of a siren fills the air. Sweat trickles down the back of my neck as I slow down and prepare to pull over.

Angel taps furiously into her phone as I put the car into park and turn off the engine.

"I told Mick what you did," she hisses in my face. "Say one thing out of line in the next few minutes, and your beautician gal pal dies. You're going to tell the officer you just found out your mother's been rushed to hospital."

I watch with bated breath as she slides the gun behind her back. It's the first time I've been free of the threat of imminent death since I pulled out of my garage. I chew on my bottom lip nervously as I wait for the officer to appear at my window. I could tell him everything and maybe save myself, but would I be trading my best friend's life for mine in the process? Without knowing Mick's location, he'll be free to hunt Kelly down, or order a hit on her. I have no doubt he knows how to get the job done—he managed to pull it off overseas.

Angel opens the glove box and grabs the car registration,

then reaches for my purse on the floor and rummages around for my driver's license. "I don't make idle threats," she warns me as she hands me the items.

I watch in my rearview mirror as the police officer climbs out of his vehicle and approaches my car. I'm not about to follow Angel's playbook and tell him a sob story to persuade him to let me off with a warning for erratic driving. It's time to make a play of my own.

"Afternoon, ma'am. I assume you know why I pulled you over?"

I give an offhanded shrug. "Bet you can't wait to tell me."

"Speeding and reckless driving. Driver's license and registration, please."

I let out a snort of disgust. "I don't have to give you my ID. I'm a sovereign citizen—"

"I'm *so* sorry, officer," Angel interrupts, leaning over and smiling apologetically at him. "My friend's mother has been rushed to the hospital. She was in a hurry to get there. She's extremely distraught as you can imagine." She elbows me sharply. "Give the officer your information."

The tremor in my hand betrays me as I hand over the paperwork.

He eyes me warily. "You seem agitated. Have you been drinking?"

"I'm agitated because you pulled me over, you jerk!" I yell, slamming the palm of my hand down on the horn and holding it there. "I need you to get out of my way. This is an unlawful stop." I turn the key in the ignition and attempt to roll up the window.

"Okay, ma'am, I'm gonna need you to step out of the vehicle," the officer says, reaching for his gun. His radio crackles to life as he calls for backup.

Assuming a scowl, I turn the car off. I've never in my life

been so thankful to undo my seatbelt and exit my car. Feigning resentment, I blink back tears of relief as I'm handcuffed.

"Is this really necessary, officer?" Angel intervenes. "My friend's under a lot of stress and you're using unnecessary force. What's your name and badge number?"

"You too, ma'am, out of the car," the officer replies abruptly. He's red in the face now—clearly, he's had enough of being badgered.

"Why? I haven't done anything," she protests, one hand sliding surreptitiously behind her back.

In a flash, the officer draws his gun on her. "Put your hands up! Get 'em up! *Now!*"

Angel slowly raises her hands in surrender, but the minute the officer begins conversing again on his radio, she opens the car door and takes off running down the embankment. My head is pounding from when she whacked me with the gun. I blink to clear my vision, only half-listening as the officer informs backup over the radio that Angel took off. Moments later, I hear the whine of sirens, and everything begins to spin around me. My knees give way and the next thing I know, I'm sliding down the door of the squad car.

WHEN I COME TO, I'm lying on a hospital bed, the morning sun streaming through the window. I make a half-hearted attempt to sit up, wincing at the pain in my head.

"Abby!" Kelly jumps up from a nearby chair, her eyes roving anxiously over my face. "Are you okay?"

I consider the question for a moment before answering. I've been cracked on the head, knifed in the shoulder, whacked on the hip, and I'm bruised and scraped up from fainting on the side of the road. *Okay* might be a stretch, but I'm alive, and so's Kelly, and that's all that matters. "I hurt all over. How long have I been here?"

"Since yesterday. You have a concussion." Kelly pulls a chair over to my bedside. "I should have insisted on driving you to the youth facility."

"It wouldn't have changed anything. They would have found another opportunity to nab me." I frown, thinking back over everything that happened. "Did they catch Angel?"

"Yes, she's in custody. I don't know about Mick. Detective Hurley said he would be in touch at some point today."

"Does Brynn know what happened?"

Kelly flattens her glossed lips into a disapproving line. "She was more concerned about why her tennis shoes didn't show up yesterday."

My phone buzzes and I try to sit up before sinking back on my pillows. "Can you answer that for me?" I ask, gesturing to my purse on the bedside locker.

Kelly fishes out my phone and hits the speaker button.

"Hello," I say, my voice sounding as frail as I feel.

"Detective Hurley here. I have some good news," he begins. "Angel's talking in exchange for partial immunity. She gave up Mick's location and we picked him up a couple of hours ago. Turns out, he hired his cousin in Ireland to abduct Declan. I contacted Walsh and it's a solid lead. The guy's done several stints in jail on various charges. They've arrested him, along with two other men."

I press my fingertips to my lips, my breath catching. "Did Angel give you any other details? Did she say ... how Declan died?"

"She claims Mick's cousin and a couple of his cronies beat Declan up to make the video more persuasive, and they took it too far. He succumbed to his injuries, and they threw his body over the cliff to try and cover up the crime."

It's no surprise to hear what I already suspected, but the pain cuts through my heart all the same—made worse by the guilt I feel. How could I ever have doubted Declan's love for me?

"We also got a search warrant for Angel's and Mick's house," Hurley continues. "We found enough incriminating evidence to indict them, including deleted emails discussing their plans."

A relieved sob slips through my lips. Kelly takes my hand and squeezes it gently.

"That's not all," Hurley adds. "Angel also confessed to participating in Tonya Myer's abduction. Her lawyer is working on a plea deal in exchange for her testifying against Mick in April Monet's aka Lynelle Cafferty's murder."

I bite back a whimper as the tears begin trickling down my face. "So this is it," I manage to choke out. "It's over."

"It would appear so," Hurley replies. "The case against you has officially been dismissed. Mick will be going away for a long time, and Angel will serve time too after the details of her plea deal are worked out." He clears his throat. "She tried to claim Brynn came to her with the idea to abduct Declan—typical deflection tactic. She would have said and done anything in that interview room to avoid as much jail time as possible." Hurley ends the call with a promise to keep me updated as things unfold.

I smile weakly across at Kelly. "They got them—both of them."

"All *three* of them," she corrects me.

"Oh yeah, I forgot—the cousin in Ireland too."

"I'm talking about Brynn," Kelly says, narrowing her eyes. "I tried to warn you she was dangerous. I believe her biological mother even if the police don't. It was all her idea from the beginning."

EPILOGUE

Declan's been gone a year already. I never imagined I'd come back here to the west coast of Ireland, but I decided I wanted to scatter some flowers from the cliff top trail into the untamed Atlantic Ocean on what would have been our first anniversary—a year that was stolen from us. A lifetime together glimpsed and gone. Is it better to have loved and lost? I'm not sure how to answer that—my grief's still too raw. Not to mention the PTSD I'm struggling with.

It was different when I lost Eric to cancer. People can relate so much better to that kind of universal loss. It's a battle we've all waged, either personally, or from the sidelines. In contrast, the horrific details of Declan's death are deeply uncomfortable—a disturbing reminder that reality sometimes converges with the most shocking of crimes we like to pretend only ever happen in movies.

Kelly and I park in the trailhead lot and begin walking along the cliff top trail in companionable silence. She's been blown away at how beautiful the west coast of Ireland is. I'm thankful she agreed to come with me on this trip. She has always been a rock of friendship in my life, and I need her support today, more than ever, as I say one final goodbye to Declan.

A group of exuberant Italian students go by, and I smile sadly at them, waiting for them to pass before I pull out the dozen red roses I picked up in town. The last thing I want to do is inflict my sadness on their enjoyment of such a breathtaking vista. I trace a fingertip over the soft velvet of the rose petals, trying to remember the outline of Declan's cheek beneath my touch. So many little details are already fuzzy. No one ever tells you that time steals before it heals.

I won't come back here again. I'm closing the book on what was supposed to be my second start full of happiness and promise—the beginning of a new life with my new husband. I don't hold what happened to Declan against this beautiful land. The depravity of the human heart is everywhere—crossing oceans, tarnishing even the young. It makes me more thankful for the kindhearted souls in this world like Walsh, and the innocent ones like Shane.

Kelly and I visited with the Murphys last night, and I thanked them again for all the kindness they showed me last year. They even insisted on refunding the Airbnb charges although I know they need the money. Shane kept stuttering how sorry he was, and I made the effort to assure him I'd forgiven him. He knew he'd done something wrong, but I don't think he grasped how consequential his actions were.

Moving on won't be easy but it's up to me to forge a new path going forward in this journey of life—to rise from the ashes for a third time. I ended up adopting a shelter dog—a black Lab named Bessie—and she's been the best thing to happen to me all year. I've also started writing a book on grief to encourage others who are forced to take this painful journey. I've already been invited to speak at a couple of small events to share my story of overcoming tragedy and adversity. The media made the honeymoon murder into a twisted fairytale of sorts, and it continues to fascinate the public. If I can use that for good, I will.

In the end, the decision to turn Brynn in for her other crimes wasn't mine to make. To sweeten her plea deal, Angel confessed to coaching Brynn on how to obtain a fraudulent identity and set up a bank account. The police got a search warrant for my house and found the journal and bank statement hidden under Brynn's mattress. As I feared would happen, she racked up several additional charges as a result, but thankfully, Clive Barrington proved to be every bit the tenacious defense attorney Sophie assured me he would be. He even managed to persuade the judge to allow Brynn to serve her time in a wilderness youth reform camp where she's subject to intensive therapy on a daily basis.

So far, she has refused any contact with me, but I haven't given up on her. I send her cards and write to her on a regular basis. She's not allowed a cell phone, but I keep hoping, one day, I'll open the mailbox to discover a letter of apology from her. She's only seventeen—she can still turn her life around with the right mindset if she chooses to. Life is all about choices and being accountable to them.

Her release date is fast approaching but the reports from the reform camp are ambivalent—multiple code violations, noncompliant behavior, adeptness at manipulating staff.

I dream of a day when she'll want to call me mom and I'll be proud to call her daughter.

Until then, I'll be watching my back.

A QUICK FAVOR

Dear Reader,

I hope you enjoyed reading *While She Slept* as much as I enjoyed writing it. Thank you for taking the time to check out my books and I would appreciate it from the bottom of my heart if you would leave a review, long or short, on Amazon as it makes a HUGE difference in helping new readers find the series. Thank you!

To be the first to hear about my  upcoming book releases, sales, and fun giveaways, sign up for my newsletter at **www.normahinkens.com** and follow me on Twitter, Instagram and Facebook. Feel free to email me at norma@normahinkens.com with any feedback or comments. I LOVE hearing from readers. YOU are the reason I keep going through the tough times.

All my best,

Norma

WHAT TO READ NEXT

Ready for another thrilling read with shocking twists and a mind-blowing murder plot?

Check out my entire lineup of thrillers on Amazon or at www.normahinkens.com.

Do you enjoy reading across genres? I also write young adult science fiction and fantasy thrillers. You can find out more about those titles at **www.normahinkens.com.**

ALL BUT SAFE

*All But Safe, the first book in the **Wicked Ways Collection*** releases November 2023.

Am I scaring you yet?

Already a father to a four-year-old daughter with his ex-wife, Cash makes a spur-of-the-moment decision to marry his girlfriend of five months, Lexi, when she unexpectedly falls pregnant.

Three weeks later, still in the throes of newlywed bliss, Lexi is brutally attacked in an underground parking garage, resulting in the tragic loss of their baby.

Freshly discharged from the hospital, she returns home to find her car spray-painted with a horrifying message from someone threatening to finish the job: *next time the knife goes through your heart.*

It's the beginning of a nightmarish chain of events that won't end well. As a dangerous net of harassment tightens, Lexi begins to question everyone around her, including her new husband.

Can she unravel the chilling web of lies her life has become before it's too late?

- A high-octane thriller with a spellbinding cast of characters and a breathtaking twist! -

BIOGRAPHY

NYT and USA Today bestselling author Norma Hinkens writes twisty psychological suspense thrillers, as well as fast-paced science fiction and fantasy about spunky heroines and epic adventures in dangerous worlds. She's also a travel junkie, legend lover, and idea wrangler, in no particular order. She grew up in Ireland, land of storytelling and the original little green man.

Find out more about her books on her website.
www.normahinkens.com

Follow her on Facebook for funnies, giveaways, cool stuff & more!

BOOKS BY N. L. HINKENS

BROWSE THE ENTIRE CATALOG AT
www.normahinkens.com/books

VILLAINOUS VACATIONS COLLECTION

- The Cabin Below
- You Will Never Leave
- Her Last Steps

DOMESTIC DECEPTIONS COLLECTION

- Never Tell Them
- I Know What You Did
- The Other Woman

PAYBACK PASTS COLLECTION

- The Class Reunion
- The Lies She Told
- Right Behind You

TREACHEROUS TRIPS COLLECTION

- Wrong Exit
- The Invitation
- While She Slept

WICKED WAYS COLLECTION

- All But Safe

NOVELLAS

- The Silent Surrogate

BOOKS BY NORMA HINKENS

I also write young adult science fiction and fantasy thrillers under Norma Hinkens.

www.normahinkens.com/books

THE UNDERGROUNDERS SERIES
POST-APOCALYPTIC

- Immurement
- Embattlement
- Judgement

THE EXPULSION PROJECT
SCIENCE FICTION

- Girl of Fire
- Girl of Stone
- Girl of Blood

Books by Norma Hinkens

THE KEEPERS CHRONICLES
EPIC FANTASY

- Opal of Light
- Onyx of Darkness
- Opus of Doom

FOLLOW NORMA

FOLLOW NORMA:

Sign up for her newsletter:
https://normahinkens.com/
Website:
https://normahinkens.com/books
Facebook:
https://www.facebook.com/NormaHinkensAuthor/
Twitter
https://twitter.com/NormaHinkens
Instagram
https://www.instagram.com/normahinkensauthor/
Pinterest:
https://www.pinterest.com/normahinkens/

Made in United States
North Haven, CT
01 August 2023

39797840R00168